"Isn't He T......ble Litt.. ..oy?"

Lynda looked over at the serious Rico. "He said my name."

Rico shook his head. "No, he didn't."

"Yes, he did," she insisted. "Didn't you hear him say 'Lynda'?"

"He isn't saying your name. He only speaks Spanish. *Linda* means pretty in Spanish. He's saying you're pretty."

The two adults looked at each other in silence as the toddler clapped his hands in the air. Rico felt a sudden pressure on his chest at the sight of Lynda standing there holding the boy, her face streaked with chocolate, her hair sticky and the front of her blouse soiled. She was neither untouchable nor remote.

He found himself wanting to wrap his arms around both the woman and the child. His stomach clenched with a powerful longing, all the more startling for its unexpectedness.

Dear Reader:

Welcome to Silhouette Desire – provocative, compelling, contemporary love stories written by and for today's woman. These are stories to treasure.

Each and every Silhouette Desire is a wonderful romance in which the emotional and the sensual go hand in hand. When you open a Desire, you enter a whole new world – a world that has, naturally, a perfect hero just waiting to whisk you away! A Silhouette Desire can be light-hearted or serious, but it will always be satisfying.

We hope you enjoy this Silhouette today – and will go on to enjoy many more.

Please write to us:

Jane Nicholls
Silhouette Books
PO Box 236
Thornton Road
Croydon
Surrey
CR9 3RU

AUDRA ADAMS
HOME SWEET HOME

Silhouette Desire

Originally Published by Silhouette Books
a division of
Harlequin Enterprises Ltd.

First published in Great Britain in 1992 by Silhouette Books, Eton House, 18-24 Paradise Road, Richmond, Surrey TW9 1SR

© Marie D. Tracy 1992

Silhouette, Silhouette Desire and Colophon are Trade Marks of Harlequin Enterprises B.V.

ISBN 0 373 58604 3

22-9207

Made and printed in Great Britain

AUDRA ADAMS

loves to dream up her characters' stories while lying on the beach on hot summer days. Luckily, her Jersey-shore home offers her the opportunity to indulge in her fantasies.

She believes that falling in love is one of the most memorable experiences in a person's life. Young or old, male or female, we all can relate to those exquisitely warm feelings. She knows that stories of romance enable us to tap into that hidden pleasure and relive it through the characters.

An incurable romantic, Audra is in love with love, and hopes to share that optimism with each and every one of her readers.

Other Silhouette Books by Audra Adams

Silhouette Desire

Blue Chip Bride
People Will Talk

For my father, Nunzio Morriale, 1910-1991

One

"**I** won't do it."

"Rico, be reasonable. Home Sweet Home needs the money."

"The money, yes. The woman, no."

Rico Alvarez turned from his friend, Steve Ballinger, and assessed the pile of mail on his desk. Mostly bills. The dilapidated leather chair protested as he slumped back and swung away from the stack of envelopes. He turned to glance out the bay window of his office.

Steve rose and paced in front of the desk. "How can you say that? You don't even know her."

Rico smirked and made a disparaging sound as he studied the scene outside his window. The air was still as waves of heat rose from the walkway. It was more than unseasonably warm this spring day, even for southern Florida.

"I know her type."

Rico leaned forward and played with the controls of the rickety air-conditioning unit, then gave up when only the same tepid air wafted in his direction. He unbuttoned the top button of his white shirt, loosened his tie and rolled up his sleeves.

Steve blew out a frustrated breath. "Don't judge everyone by Justine Twyman. That happened long ago and far away."

"And a lesson well learned," Rico added.

"You're letting a bad past experience cloud your better judgment. You should be thinking of the shelter, the kids, not your own personal hang-up."

"You're a social worker, Steve, not a psychologist. Save the analysis for someone who needs it. The fact remains that I won't schmooze with some old society matron and that's final."

"Will you listen to me? She's not—"

"Rico!" Mrs. Ortiz, the housekeeper, poked her head through the office doorway. "Come quick! The kitchen sink again."

Rico muttered a curse under his breath, then grabbed the toolbox from the corner of his office. He followed the housekeeper down the hall and into the kitchen, with Steve trailing close behind.

"See what I mean?" Steve jumped back to avoid the steady stream of water that spouted from the pipe under the sink. "This place is literally falling apart at the seams. Health and Human Services is going to close you down with the next inspection, and then where will the kids be?"

Rico studied the leaking pipe, then wrapped a rag around the joint as he sorted through the toolbox in search of a wrench.

"Tell me something I don't know."

He knelt down on the soggy towels Mrs. Ortiz had placed in front of the sink to mop up the water and stuck his head into the cabinet under the sink. The housekeeper silently handed Rico the tools as needed in a manner much like a nurse-to-surgeon operating procedure. They'd been this route before.

"Won't you even meet her?" Steve poked his head down into the opening.

"You're in my light," Rico said, readjusting his body so that he was half-in, half-out of the cabinet.

Steve moved. "Well, how about it?"

"Can we talk about this later, please? I'm a little busy now." A splash of water slapped him in the face, and he rubbed the back of his hand to wipe his eyes, leaving a smear of grease across his forehead.

"I think we should settle this right away. You really need to talk to her now."

Rico cursed the tight space as he caught his thumb in the wrench. He brought the finger to his mouth. "What is it with you and this rich broad, huh, Steve? Why in hell do we have to deal with this right now?"

Steve's not-too-discreet cough was the only answer. "Well?"

"Perhaps because the 'rich broad' is standing here right now?" said a decidedly feminine voice, reminiscent of a young Lauren Bacall.

Rico's hand froze in midmotion. He shifted his body and peered out between the pipes.

The first thing he saw was her legs. They were long and sleek with expensive hose—even in this heat. The bottom half of her white linen dress stopped slightly above the knee, but hinted at limbs that went on forever.

Rico slowly extricated himself from his awkward position under the sink. In one fluid motion, he was on his feet, slightly worse for the wear. He gave only a passing glance to Steve's victorious smirk. His attention was riveted on the woman before him.

As he examined her, she stood tall, adjusting her dress before tugging the lapels of the matching hip-length jacket.

Cool. Blond. Rich. The three thoughts coalesced and became one.

Rico took a small step back and leaned against the counter. It seemed the wise thing to do.

Steve grinned. "Richard Alvarez, I'd like you to meet Lynda St. Clair."

Lynda extended her hand. "It's a pleasure to meet you, Mr. Alvarez. I've heard so much about you."

Rico took her hand in his. It was small, warm and perfectly manicured. "Mrs. St. Clair," he said, "I think I owe you an apology."

She laughed. "Because of the 'broad' remark? That's quite all right." She turned to charm Steve with her smile. "I don't think anyone has ever called me that. At least not to my face."

"Why don't we go into my office," Rico said. Steve took hold of Lynda's arm and led her toward the hallway. Rico turned toward Mrs. Ortiz. "You can use the sink, but not at full force. I'll finish up later."

Lynda sat down in Rico's office and watched as he wiped his hands on a clean towel. He rolled down his sleeves and put his jacket on. Lynda was nervous, but she knew she hid it well. She was a master at maintaining a cool, reserved exterior at those times in life when all hell was breaking loose inside.

Times like now.

He wasn't quite what she'd expected. Somehow she had pictured an older man, with white hair and a sunny disposition. He was certainly not that. She estimated late thirties as she studied his defined features. The combination of his big, dark eyes and black wavy hair contrasted sharply with the stark whiteness of his shirt. His face was intense; he didn't look as if he laughed much.

And then there was the earring—a small gold stud discreetly pierced through his left earlobe.

Funny that Dee had never said a word about his being handsome. It was totally unlike her not to mention such a thing. Though Dee and Steve were happily married, she never failed to appreciate another healthy, good-looking male...and Richard Alvarez was certainly that.

He was a bit taller than average with those dark, sensuous looks one only seemed to see on television, never in real life.

"Lynda, why don't you start by telling Rico what you can do for the shelter," Steve said.

Lynda looked at Rico. A serious scowl graced his face, and she wondered what he was thinking. She could tell he was going to be a hard sell. But she'd dealt with skeptics before, and she'd proved them wrong.

"Well, I'm not really prepared to go into a major presentation on a specific fund-raising program for Home Sweet Home." She looked at Rico. "We'll have to discuss your needs first, of course. But I can tell you what Events, Inc. does, if you wish."

"I'm more interested in what *I* have to do, Mrs. St. Clair."

"Ms."

"All right. *Ms.* St. Clair," he said, a curt nod acknowledging her correction. "What I'm interested in is how disruptive this process is going to be to me, the shelter and most of all the children."

"We try to work within your schedule. You tell us when it's convenient," Lynda said.

"Lynda, why don't you explain the program," Steve said.

"The program can be minimal or elaborate, depending on how much money you need to raise."

"A lot," Rico said, his eyes locking with Lynda's.

"Okay, elaborate. That will involve a full program including a promotional film about the shelter, a journal illustrating your work here in which we sell donor pages, and culminating in a dinner-dance event."

"How involved will I have to be personally?" Rico asked.

"That depends on how personally involved you are with Home Sweet Home," Lynda said.

Steve laughed. "Rico *is* Home Sweet Home. There wouldn't be a shelter without him. He owns it, operates it and deals with the devil to keep it open."

"Then it's safe to say you're very involved," Lynda added.

"Intimately," Rico stated, his dark eyes penetrating her cool facade.

Lynda expelled a long-held breath. "If that's true, I'm afraid you will have to be the focal point around which the program is planned. We're selling a product here, Mr. Alvarez, and the way I see it, that product is *you.*"

Rico stood and walked around the desk toward the door.

"I thank you for your time, Ms. St. Clair. It's been very enlightening."

Both Steve and Lynda stood.

"Rico—"

"No." Rico put up his hand to Steve. "I told you before I wasn't interested, but you insisted. I'm sorry you wasted your time, Ms. St. Clair, but this is not the way for me to go."

"But you do need the money," she said.

"I'll find it. I always have."

"I really haven't had a chance to explain. You may not understand how these things work—"

"You don't have to," Rico said. "I *have* been to charity events before, Ms. St. Clair. The welfare of the children is my primary concern. I don't want them paraded around like poster children. They've been through enough already." He held open the office door. "Now, if you don't mind, the school children will be home soon."

Lynda and Steve exchanged appraising glances. Lynda took a card out of her bag and handed it to Rico. "If you should change your mind."

He didn't take it from her.

"I won't."

Steve was about to say something, but the look in Rico's eyes seemed to change his mind. He shook his head. "I'll call you tomorrow."

After a polite goodbye, Rico sent them on their way. Lynda followed Steve out onto the pebblestone driveway. She brushed off his apologies for wasting her time, and she promised to call Dee soon. She waved to him as he drove off.

Lynda sat in the car in silence as the afternoon sun beat down on her through the windshield. She didn't start the engine or turn on the air conditioning, but stared instead at the condition of the old Victorian house. She was more than disappointed. Dee had said the shelter needed help, but by the looks of the place, that was an understatement.

She took a deep breath and blew it out slowly. It didn't matter what the place looked like. It was the work inside that counted, not the surroundings. She thought about Rico Alvarez and his determination not to get involved with her, and found that she couldn't accept defeat so easily.

She'd run herself ragged these past few years building Events, Inc. into a premier fund-raising organization. She was good at what she did. No. She was the best. Her life had been her training ground, and nobody could turn the charm on better than she to get what she wanted.

When her husband had left her, she'd thought she'd lost everything, her identity included. Events, Inc. had been born of desperation, but now it was her shining star. She was proud of the programs she planned, the people and worthy charities she'd helped, and it stuck in her craw that someone like Rico Alvarez would turn her down before he even gave her a chance.

And she was sure it was *she* he didn't want to work with. If someone—anyone—else had walked through that door today, his response would have been positive. He had been testing her all through the interview, but she hadn't the vaguest idea for what. One thing was certain, he didn't trust her, and he was using his distrust as the reason for his rejection.

Lynda opened the car door and stepped out. She checked her watch. Rico said that the children who attended school would be arriving home soon. She wanted to get back inside and deal with him one-on-one, without Steve or anyone else around.

She wanted this job, but not for the money it would bring Events, Inc. Though she'd refused alimony from Phillip, she was more than comfortable. She didn't need money. She needed work, purpose and a reason to live. Helping these children was by far the best reason she had come across to date.

The doorbell rang at the same time all hell broke loose in the hallway. Rico stepped out of his office to hear Mrs. Ortiz spew a litany of threats in Spanish as she chased after a wide-eyed, sticky-fingered child. The woman paused long enough only to swing open the front door before she disappeared around the bend after the toddler.

"Hello again."

Rico spun around at the sound of her voice. She stood framed in the brightly lit doorway, the yellow sun at her back.

"Did you forget something?" he asked.

"No. I came back to talk."

"I can't see what else there is to say," he answered.

"Why don't you like me, Mr. Alvarez?"

Rico moved into the hallway and stuffed his hands into his pants pocket. "I don't know you well enough to like or dislike you, Ms. St. Clair."

"Then why won't you give me a chance to help?"

"I think the question should be 'why do you want to help?'" he said.

"It's my business. It's what I do for a living."

"Ah," he said. "So you do this for money."

"No."

"Then why?"

"To give something back. To get something in return. Surely you of all people can understand that."

Rico nodded. Yes, he knew all about that. But it wasn't in his experience to believe she did.

"You don't believe me, do you?" Lynda asked.

"It doesn't matter what I believe or don't believe. I'm not going to exploit the children for the benefit of the shelter."

"What if I promised you I wouldn't do that?"

"I don't see how you can avoid it."

"Trust me."

"Give me one good reason why I should," he said.

"Give me one good reason why you shouldn't," she answered.

Rico managed a half grin. "Touché."

"I'll make a deal with you," she said, hand on hip. "Show me around the shelter, and I'll come up with a preliminary plan free of charge that you can approve or disapprove."

Rico studied her for a long moment. What was she up to? Why didn't she just leave? This was his problem, not hers.

"Come on," she urged. "What have you got to lose? Do it for the kids. Think of what they need."

"You have no idea what they need. These are the throwaways of society, Ms. St. Clair. The children of neglect."

"Neglect has many faces, Mr. Alvarez," Lynda said.

Perhaps it was the words themselves, or the way she said them, but Rico felt a tug somewhere deep inside. He was curious as to how a woman such as this could have any experience with neglect, but then, she was right, neglect had many faces.

"All right," Rico said with a somewhat reluctant nod. "I'll give you the 'Cook's tour' of the place tomorrow morning. But no promises."

Lynda smiled broadly. "No promises," she agreed, but she was elated. She felt as if she'd just gone fifteen rounds and had been declared a winner by a TKO. She was exhausted, but exhilarated.

"Till tomorrow," Lynda said, and extended her hand.

Rico took her hand in his and gave it a gentle squeeze. "Tomorrow."

He ushered her to the door and watched her carefully maneuver around the cracked and crumbling walkway. The afternoon rays of the sun caught and tangled in her hair, creating a golden aura around her head. He was mesmerized for the briefest of moments before catching himself.

He knew all about her; not who she was, of course, but *what* she was. He'd met hundreds like her over the past five years, since he'd become involved with the shelter. Society debs and matrons arrived at all hours of the day or night, dressed to kill, checkbook in hand, ready to do their part for "noblesse oblige."

He didn't mind. He needed them, and every dime he could guilt out of them. After a quick tour of the shelter, they'd be on their way with their designer bags somewhat lighter and their consciences assuaged, secure in the knowledge that they'd once again helped those poor, underprivileged children.

A wry smile crossed his face. Contrary to what Steve had said before, he didn't hate her kind. He'd stopped feeling that useless emotion years ago. It wasted too much time, too much energy—energy better directed

toward those who'd come to count on him for their
very survival.

He thought about Justine, another blonde whose
blood had been as hot as it had been blue. She'd
picked him up in her sleek red Cadillac and had taken
him for a ride in more ways than one. At the tender
age of nineteen, he'd learned all about the real world
of the haves and the have-nots. She'd told him she
loved him, and he'd sure as hell thought he loved her,
but when it came right down to it, she outclassed him
three-to-one. He had been hurt and bitter for a long
time after that; had dropped out of college, gone to
'Nam. Time had dulled, then numbed the ache, but
the sight of any other cool, sophisticated blonde never
failed to conjure up the memory.

Rico stepped back from the doorway and admired
Ms. St. Clair more fully as she slid behind the wheel
of her cream-colored Mercedes. He had to admit he
did like the way she moved—slowly, steadily, like a
frosty lemon ice melting on a hot summer day. His
throat went dry at the thought, and he swallowed before moving back into the house and closing the door.

Not for you, Rico. Out of your league. Way out.

Two

___

Bright and early the next morning, Lynda arrived at the doorstep of Home Sweet Home. At least she'd thought it was bright and early. By the looks of the place, it seemed more like Grand Central Station at rush hour. Children of various ages and sizes milled about the hallway in organized chaos as they selected their books, lunch bags and backpacks. They stared at her with curiosity as they headed out the door. She managed to exchange a greeting or two before she was almost knocked over in the mad dash toward the waiting school bus.

After discovering Rico's office empty, Lynda walked down toward the kitchen area in search of an adult. As she passed the door on her left, it swung open.

"Are you the new aide? Please say yes!"

Lynda turned to stare at the tall redhead with the oversize apron who didn't bother to wait for her answer.

"I'm Debbie Marshall, the nursery school teacher. Today's finger-painting day, and my helper didn't show up."

"I'm Lynda St. Clair. I'm working on a plan for a fund-raiser for Home Sweet Home."

"Then you're not the aide?"

"Afraid not," Lynda said.

"That's too bad." Debbie sighed. "You'll have to excuse me. Since our funding was cut, I've fallen into this bad habit of jumping on any warm adult body that happens to pass my door. Sorry to bother you." She waved and headed back inside the den.

Lynda smiled at her back as she retreated. She seemed nice—young, energetic and definitely involved in her work. The kitchen was empty when she checked; Mrs. Ortiz was nowhere in sight. Lynda browsed around a bit, then poked her head inside the large room adjacent to the kitchen.

Debbie was hunched over one of the two small wooden worktables in the center of the room. She looked up when Lynda walked in behind her.

"I don't mean to interrupt," Lynda said. "But since Mr. Alvarez isn't around right now, I have some free time. I'd be glad to help out if you want."

Debbie laughed. "Silly question! Grab an apron behind the door over there. The little ones will be in any minute. There are only six of them, but...well, you'll see what I mean!"

Lynda donned a long beige apron, which covered her blouse and skirt. She was dressed more casually than yesterday, hoping she would seem less threatening to the children ... and Rico as well.

Her thoughts were interrupted by a rumbling sound that vibrated through the room. She looked at Debbie as the floorboards began to shake.

"What's that?" she asked.

"The pitter-patter of tiny feet. Brace yourself. Here they come!"

As the door swung open, six little bodies threw themselves into the room, each seeming to run off in a different direction. Lynda grabbed hold of a little boy who lost no time in climbing onto the top of the table. Once she had him seated, she took off after another who resembled the little one Mrs. Ortiz had chased yesterday. He seemed to recognize her, too, and proceeded to cling to her leg so tightly she had to walk with him attached ball-and-chain style.

Debbie barked out a series of orders, and within ten minutes or so, the two women had each child covered with a smock and sitting on a bench seat ready to go to work.

It was fun. More fun that she could have ever imagined. She worked with three children, and Debbie worked with three, then they switched. Some of the pictures the children made were bright, colorful; others were grim and somber.

By studying their faces as they worked, Lynda could almost predict which children would paint what pictures.

"What a pretty flower!" Lynda said as she leaned over a girl with long blond hair the same shade as hers. "Is your name Suzy?"

The little girl nodded and shyly showed off her picture. It was a bright yellow daisy with a red center, but it stood all alone on the page.

"Why don't you add some green grass down here and a sun up in the sky?" Lynda suggested and brought the appropriate paint containers within the girl's reach.

"No." Suzy shook her head emphatically.

"Why not? That poor little flower looks too lonely all by itself."

"It's a bad flower," Suzy said in a thick Southern accent.

Lynda waited for her to continue, but it was soon evident that Suzy felt her answer said it all. As Lynda looked into her melancholy blue eyes, she had to agree that perhaps it did.

Lynda couldn't think of anything further to say to the girl. These were special children with special needs. The thought took all the air out of her sails. Maybe Rico *was* right, maybe she had no idea what these children needed. He'd called them the "throwaways of society," and she, after all, appeared to be the embodiment of that very society.

Was that why he resented her so much? Did she represent to him all the things that were wrong with the world? If that was so, she had an extremely formidable task ahead of her.

"How are we doing?" Debbie asked as she came up behind her. "Oh, Suzy, what a beautiful flower! I love it, don't you, Lynda? Let's hang it on the door as soon as it dries, okay?"

Suzy smiled and nodded, handing her painting over to Debbie before scurrying off to the other table for her snack.

"This is a breakthrough, believe it or not," Debbie said to Lynda as she held up the picture of the flower. "When Suzy first came here, she wouldn't even pick up a pencil. All she did was sit in the corner with her head in her hands. Now she joins in. The improvement has been remarkable."

"She seems so sad."

"She is. They all are," Debbie said with a sweep of her hand. "Patrick over there was abused. He only paints black. He never works with any other color. He used to cover the entire paper with black paint, corner to corner. Last week was the first time he left an open spot on the page. When I pointed it out to him, he said, 'It's a window.'" Debbie's mouth turned up with a half smile. "It's a start."

"I didn't know what to say to her," Lynda admitted.

"Don't worry about that. Just praise her. Suzy and the others are going through a healing process that only time can help. We all do what we can. It's hard at first, but you can't blame yourself." Debbie taped the picture to the door. "You can't dwell on what they've been through. When you work with children like these, you have to remember that you're not part of the problem, you're part of the solution."

A fight broke out at the snack table, as two boys grabbed the same cookie. The women immediately ran over to pull them apart. Lynda grabbed hold of Tomás, the sticky-fingered toddler from yesterday, who, it seemed, had taken a fancy to her. She wet a washcloth and proceeded to clean him up and calm him down.

That was the way Rico found her when he entered the room. She was on her knees in front of the boy, gently wiping his hands and face, and speaking to him in soft tones. He couldn't hear what she was saying, but then, he didn't have to. The look on her face said it all.

He was a little surprised to see her today. She'd said she'd be here, but he was sure that once she'd thought about it, she'd change her mind and decide it wasn't worth the bother. But here she was, on time while he was late, obviously pitching in to help if the apron and the smear of red paint on her cheek were any indication.

Despite himself, Rico was becoming increasingly curious as to exactly who and what Ms. St. Clair really was.

Lynda looked up and their eyes met. For a breath of a moment, they just stared at each other. She felt the power of his black eyes pull at her, and her heart began to pound.

And then he smiled. A broad smile, the first she'd seen.

What a strange, complex man, she thought, not without some trepidation. She'd met some very important, powerful people in her life—a king included—but none of them had ever evoked such a strong response in her. Rico was compelling, mesmerizing, and more than a little bit frightening. In many ways, she supposed, he was as alien to her as any foreign dignitary. His world and hers were far apart, farther than could be measured in the miles between Miami and Palm Beach.

Her instincts told her that she should run, but like a moth to a flame, all she wanted to do was fly closer.

''Hi,'' she said.

"Hi." Rico walked closer to her and Tomás. He said something to the boy in Spanish, and the toddler smiled and ran off.

"He's sweet," Lynda said as she stood.

"He's a devil." Rico grinned after him. "But he's one of my favorites." He turned to look at her. "Are you ready for your tour?"

"All set." Lynda shrugged out of the apron and hung it back on the hook.

"Haven't changed your mind about this?"

Lynda shook her head. "Not on your life."

Rico raised his eyebrows at her adamant remark, but didn't comment.

"Then..." He extended his arm and directed her into the kitchen.

"How many children are living at the shelter?" Lynda asked, all business now.

Rico hesitated for an imperceptible moment. "We're licensed to care for ten children at any given time."

They stood in the bright, airy room next to the large butcher-block worktable, which dominated its center. An aroma of freshly baked cake filled her nostrils.

"Mmm, chocolate. Smells delicious."

"Mrs. Ortiz is a wonderful cook. She's not only our housekeeper, but our 'mother hen' as well." Rico pointed to the back patio doors. "This is the backyard and play area. Once the older children get home at three, it gets a bit crazy out there."

"You must need a lot of help."

"Yes, and there's never enough. The cuts in our public funding have been deep, and we've had to let some people go. You've met Debbie. She teaches the preschoolers in the morning. The others are aides.

Steve lends us his expertise once a week, but most professionals won't work without getting paid."

"Yes, I know. Doreen—"

"Steve's wife? She's been a good friend to the shelter over the years. She's helped with a lot of our private fund-raising. Do you know her well?"

"Dee and I grew up together."

Rico was surprised. He knew that Dee came from a moneyed background, but she was so down-to-earth, he never gave it much thought.

"Dee is the one who told me about Home Sweet Home's problems. She suggested doing a charity dinner to raise money. Steve and I worked on an event for a senior citizens' home last year. It seemed natural to ask me to become involved here." Lynda pushed a tendril of hair behind her ear. "I didn't know you and the Ballingers were such good friends."

"Steve and I went to college together. We socialize quite a bit."

"Funny we never met before," Lynda said.

Rico smirked. "I don't think we travel in the same circles, Ms. St. Clair."

Lynda returned a level gaze, but decided not to comment. They had actually been having a decent conversation, and she was determined not to exchange barbs with him. She changed the subject.

"What's through here?" she asked.

"That's the dining room."

Lynda pushed open the swinging door to a large dining area complete with an intricately carved mahogany banquet table that had seen better days. Rico followed her gaze.

"A donation from one of our Palm Beach patrons," he said. "I'm sure that table is wondering what it did so wrong in life to deserve to end up here."

"Maybe it's thrilled to be away from all those stuffed-shirts and doing something useful for a change."

Rico studied her face and considered her cryptic remark, but remained silent as he led her through the recreation room and up the stairs to the second floor.

"The house is small. We have to bunk as many as four children to a room," he said as they entered and examined the various bedrooms.

Lynda noticed how neat and clean each room was. Each of the children had their own shelf for their personal belongings. She picked up a chipped porcelain doll with a faded mauve velvet dress. It had obviously been handmade long ago, and she admired the craftsmanship. It reminded her of a similar doll she had when she was a little girl. It had been given to her by one of the myriad nannies who had been employed over the years to care for her. The woman hadn't lasted very long in her position, and Lynda could no longer recall her name.

Rico interrupted her thoughts. "These children tend to cherish the familiar, no matter how old or worn."

"It's beautiful," Lynda said. "Someone once took great care to make it."

Lynda replaced the doll and followed Rico to the next room. Each was the same. She marveled at the organization it took to keep such a place open and running smoothly.

Rico stopped at the end of the hallway. He pushed open the door. "This is my room," he said, and waited as she entered ahead of him.

The room was small, Spartan and stiflingly hot. A twin-size bed was up against the wall in the corner. There was a nightstand next to it and a mirrored dresser across from the bed. The only window faced the front of the house and held a casement-type air conditioner.

Rico's toiletries were scattered haphazardly on top of the dresser. His subtle musk cologne permeated the humid room. Lynda breathed deeply, drawing the moist, scented air into her lungs. As she turned, she caught her reflection in the mirror. Her cheeks were flushed, her hairline damp and her lips full as if in anticipation...of what, she didn't dare ask herself.

"Not much to look at, but it keeps me upstairs near the kids at night," Rico said.

"Y-yes. That's important," she said, embarrassed by her own thoughts.

Rico came up behind her. They studied each other in the mirror. Rico knew he was staring, but couldn't help himself. She was beautiful. Her hair was pinned back, with strands falling around as it came undone. His insides tightened. The silence was resonant, its voice slowly rising to a siren's pitch. It beckoned him to come closer, to touch, taste, feel.

But that was a taboo, all the more inviolate because it was self-imposed. He was sure she had no idea how she affected him. Better that way, he told himself, better for her to be wary of him than to know.

She wouldn't be here long. Once he'd rejected her program, she'd be gone. The thought depressed him, and he pushed it aside. For the time being, he did promise her a chance.

"Seen enough?" he asked.

Lynda nodded, thankful for the reprieve—from what, she wasn't sure. The only thing she was certain of was her adolescent reaction to the powerful masculine magnetism he seemed to possess. It drew her toward him, pulled her in like a fish on a line. It clouded her mind and gave her chills at the same time. She shook her head as if to free it from a tangle of cottony webs. This confusion was not good for a working relationship with him, and a working relationship was all she wanted with any man...an *equal*, working relationship.

They set back down the stairway. The phone rang in Rico's office, and he excused himself. Lynda followed him and surveyed the cramped room as she waited for him to finish his call.

Several piles of file folders were stacked on the floor against the sole gray metal file cabinet in the corner. A scraggly-looking rhododendron teetered on the brink of death as it rested on the window seat behind his desk. The room looked in desperate need of attention, and Lynda made a mental note to get it spruced up before the film crew made the video.

That is, *if* he hired her.

Rico followed Lynda's every move as she examined his office. It didn't take a genius to know what she thought of the place, but there was never any time to file, or organize, and he wouldn't apologize for that. He wondered how much longer she'd stay. He'd already wasted too much time with her, and needed to get back to work. His attention returned to his call, and he said an abrupt "goodbye" before cradling the receiver.

"Sorry about the interruption." He walked around the desk and leaned against it. "Will there be anything else, Ms. St. Clair?"

Lynda felt the frost. His return to formality indicated most clearly that the wall had dropped again. She knew she had to come up with something that would intrigue him, or she was lost.

She stood, only a foot or so away from him. His presence was intimidating. He was a quiet man, a man of few words, but then, he didn't need them. His eyes and his body language spoke volumes.

"I'd like to do a video about the shelter."

Rico shook his head. "Ms. St.—"

"No, please. Let me finish. I want to show the house, the area, the work you do for the community. I won't dwell on the children. We'll only tape them from a distance."

"I don't think—"

"Just one afternoon. I promise that you won't even know we're here. If it turns out as I think it will, we'll be talking about a major marketing tool you could use over and over again to raise funds. Isn't that what you want?"

"Of course it is—"

"Then let me try. Please."

Rico looked into her large blue eyes. A thousand reasons why he should say "no" flashed through his brain. But those eyes were clear, honest, almost laughably "true blue," and he could feel his determination slipping. It was against his better judgment, but the more he stared into those eyes, the more he asked himself what harm it could possibly do.

"When."

Lynda's heart skipped a beat. "Next week," she said quickly before he changed his mind. "I'll call you as soon as I can set up the film crew."

He nodded.

She smiled.

Suddenly Tomás ran into the office and charged right into Lynda, almost knocking her to the floor. Lynda reached down to steady the boy, and found herself looking at a small, round face smudged with chocolate cake.

Mrs. Ortiz was close behind, rattling off a stream of steady Spanish, which Lynda supposed were reprimands to the little boy.

"Now look what you've done!" The housekeeper threw her arms up in despair. "You've ruined the nice lady's clothes. No, no, Tomás."

Lynda looked down at the chocolate stains all along the front of her skirt and laughed out loud. "It's all right," she said as she bent to lift the squirming boy. "My, you're a handful!"

"Here, let me take him," Rico held out his arms for the child, who shook his head emphatically. "It looks as if he's gotten into the cake again."

"Every day, that boy!" Mrs. Ortiz lamented. "He needs a keeper all his own! I tell you, Rico, I don't have time to run after him. And he don't nap like the others, you know? He runs like *¡diablo!*"

"He's fine, really," Lynda said. "I don't mind holding him."

Rico introduced Lynda and the housekeeper while Tomás proceeded to entwine his sticky fingers in Lynda's hair. She turned to the boy. "So, Tomás, remember me? I'm Lynda. Do you think we can be friends?"

"Linda," Tomás repeated, and rubbed his chubby palms against her cheek. *"Linda, linda."*

"Isn't he adorable?" Lynda looked over at the serious Rico. "He said my name."

Rico shook his head. "No, he didn't."

"Yes, he did," she insisted. "Didn't you hear him say 'Lynda'?"

"He isn't saying your name. He only speaks Spanish."

"But—"

"*'Linda'* means 'pretty' in Spanish. He's saying you're pretty."

"Oh," she said, strangely uncomfortable with the turn in the conversation.

"Linda," Tomás repeated.

The two adults looked at each other in silence as the toddler clapped his hands in the air. Rico felt a pressure on his chest at the sight of her standing there holding the boy, her face streaked with chocolate, her hair sticky and the front of her blouse soiled. She was neither as untouchable nor as remote as before. He found himself wanting to wrap his arms around both of them. His stomach clenched with a powerful longing, all the more startling for its unexpectedness.

It was insane. It was unlike him. He didn't give in to impulse anymore. He didn't have to fight urges because the days of strong, overpowering urges were long gone, over, done with. He'd consciously and systematically put an end to them. So why did this woman—the antithesis of all he stood for—elicit such a response in him?

Rico reached out and took Tomás from her arms. "I'll keep him with me, Mrs. Ortiz."

The housekeeper muttered to herself as she left the office and headed back to the kitchen.

Lynda took a tissue from her bag and wiped her trembling hands. She didn't look at Rico. She couldn't. Basic masculinity oozed from every pore of his body. He represented something light-years beyond her experience where men were concerned. The suit, the tie, his entire outward appearance, was a lie. This was no polite, sophisticated gentleman to whom she could relate. He was more the stalking predator, ready and able to pounce on his latest prey. Her stomach fluttered like a trapped bird as she both wondered and thrilled to the thought that she might be his next.

She tried to imagine her ex-husband, Phillip, in his place, but could not. Phillip was blond, pale, sterile in comparison to Rico. There was no one remotely like Rico in her life. She patently didn't know what to do with him.

Despite herself, her gaze locked with his. He did things with his eyes that some men might be arrested for. She felt as if he were touching her, and her body shivered with a haunting desire to know what would happen if he truly did.

"I'm sorry Tomás ruined your clothes," he said softly.

"No problem," she answered, grateful her cool facade was still intact.

The phone began to ring again.

"I'd better be going now," she said, anxious to put some distance between them. "I'll call you about the film crew."

"That will be fine."

The phone continued to ring. "You'd better answer that," she said, and headed for the door.

Rico nodded thoughtfully. He wanted to say something else to her, then thought better of it. He heard the front door shut as he reached for the phone.

"Home Sweet Home," he said into the receiver, but heard only the dial tone in return.

He cradled the phone and turned toward the window to watch Lynda as she climbed into her car. Tomás shifted in his arms, and he adjusted the boy's weight.

"*Linda,*" Tomás said, pointing toward the car as it pulled out of the driveway.

"*Sí,* Tomás," Rico said. "*Muy linda.*"

Three

Lynda aimed the VCR remote control toward the television screen. The frame froze with a head shot of Rico superimposed over the logo for Home Sweet Home.

She turned to look at Dee. "So, what do you think?"

Doreen Ballinger tilted her head toward her friend. "I was just about to ask you the same question."

"I think it's a great promotional video. The film crew did an excellent job. They hardly interfered with the operation of the shelter, just as Mr. Alvarez requested. The video shows Home Sweet Home in the best possible light without a lot of hearts and flowers."

"I'm not talking about the video," Dee said. "I'm talking about *him*. What do you think of Rico?"

Lynda stood and walked over to the television. She hit the Stop button, then rewound the tape. "I don't know what you mean."

Doreen walked up behind her. "You know perfectly well what I mean, Lynda St. Clair."

Lynda turned to Dee and looked her in the eye. "Why didn't you tell me about him?"

Dee shrugged. "What's to tell?"

"'What's to tell?' You led me to believe he was some kindly old man with the sweetest disposition in the world. 'A teddy bear,' if I remember your exact words."

Dee grinned. "So I lied."

"No kidding."

"Well, would you have agreed to take the job if I'd told you the truth?"

A picture of Rico's face flashed across Lynda's mind, and she shivered inwardly. "No," she admitted, and turned back to the machine, ejecting the rewound tape.

"See? I had no choice. They really need you for this fund-raiser. Knowing your track record with men... Don't look at me like that! You haven't been out with a man since Phillip. You left me little choice but to be evasive."

"Evasive? That's a laugh! You could have prepared me, for heaven's sake. The man almost bit my head off at the first meeting."

"I know. Steve told me. I apologize for that. But he is really very charming once you get to know him."

"I find that hard to believe." Lynda put the tape into her briefcase and picked up her jacket.

"Don't run off," Dee said. "Have a cup of tea and talk for a while."

"Okay," Lynda said, suddenly not at all anxious to rush off to the shelter. This was her last chance to sell her concept for the fund-raiser to Rico. She knew he wouldn't give her another. The video was good, but the man was difficult to please. She was at odds with herself as to how to handle him, and that fact seemed to bother her more than anything.

Lynda sat across from Dee and accepted a cup of tea. She took a sip of the hot liquid and put the cup down.

"Tell me about him."

"Rico?" Dee shook her head. "I don't have much to tell. He and Steve became friendly years ago when they both attended college at night. Steve was going for his master's, and Rico went back to get his degree. He'd dropped out, but I don't know the whole story as to why. He had just started working with his brother, Joe."

"The priest?"

"Yes. Have you met him?"

Lynda shook her head. "No, but I heard Mrs. Ortiz speaking about him." She took another sip. "Go on."

"That's really it. I don't know much more about him. He keeps to himself about his private life."

"Never married?"

"Not that I know of. He dates occasionally. Sometimes we double. But that's been a while. He's been up to his neck with the shelter this past year since the government cut his funding. I don't think he socializes much. Though not for lack of women. Every one who meets him falls all over him." Dee grinned over the rim of her teacup. "Except you, that is."

"He is good-looking, I guess," Lynda said.

"You guess? Come on, Lynda, admit it, the guy is gorgeous. You'd have to be blind not to notice."

"Okay! I noticed." Lynda stood up and walked around the sofa. She picked up her briefcase and jacket. "I really have to go."

"Don't be nervous. He'll love the video." Dee followed her to the door and gave Lynda a hug. "When do the ladies at the club screen it?"

"Tonight. Right after Rico gives me the go-ahead. I'm meeting Barbara and the rest at the club for dinner." Lynda returned the hug, a weak smile on her face. "I feel I have so much riding on this thing. I don't know why, but I really want to work on this one."

Dee gave her a Cheshire cat grin.

"And what's that supposed to mean?" Lynda asked.

"Nothing. Not a thing," Dee said innocently and gave Lynda a gentle push out the door. "Go get him."

The sun was bright overhead and steamy hot as Lynda stepped from her car in front of the shelter. It had drizzled early in the morning, and the air smelled of wet earth and freshly cut grass. She pushed back a strand of blond hair from her face, took a deep breath and rang the bell.

When no one arrived after a decent amount of time, Lynda rang again. She heard noise on the other side of the door and wondered if anyone had heard her.

She tried the knob, which turned easily. She poked her head inside.

"Hello?"

No one answered. Lynda stepped inside and shut the door behind her. Children's voices carried from up-

stairs, but Lynda made her way down the long hallway toward the kitchen. Before she reached it, the
door to the den swung open, and a young, attractive
brunette, no more than twenty, stood before her.

"Hi. Can I help you?"

"I'm Lynda St. Clair from Events, Inc. here to see
Mr. Alvarez."

The girl looked over her shoulder warily. "Uh, I
don't think now is a good time. We've—"

"Who is it, Elena?"

Lynda heard Rico's voice.

"A Lynda St. Clair, Rico. She wants you."

Lynda felt uncomfortable with the girl's choice of
words. "Just for a few minutes, tell him," she said.

Elena complied.

"Tell her, 'Not today.'"

Elena turned back to Lynda. "Sorry. Maybe you
should call him and set up an appointment."

"Elena! Let's go. I need you."

"Excuse me," Elena said, and let the door swing
shut.

Lynda was annoyed. No, more than annoyed—she
was angry. Gone was her apprehension at seeing him
again. How dare he put her off as if she were an unwelcome door-to-door salesman or something? He was
not only difficult and arrogant, but rude as well. Who
did he think he was?

She pushed open the den door, and was just about
to tell him off, when the sight that greeted her stopped
her cold.

In the center of the room sat a plastic kiddie pool,
filled with milky white water and three splashing children. Rico was on his knees on one side, with Elena on
the other, and both were soaked to the skin.

Lynda's mouth formed an O, but no words emerged.

Two children were giggling, the other was crying. It was a madhouse, and Lynda wondered if Rico had lost his mind.

"What in the world...?"

Rico looked up, then groaned.

It wasn't fair. He wasn't up to dealing with her today. His resistance was low, and what little patience he had left, he needed for the children. He shut his eyes for a minute in a vain attempt to wish her away, but when he opened them, she was still standing in the doorway.

She had no right to be here, not today with chaos reigning supreme. Not having slept straight through for three consecutive nights, he was tired, grouchy and in no mood to banter back and forth with some creamy blonde who looked as if she'd just stepped off the beach in St. Moritz.

"Chicken pox," he said abruptly.

Lynda let the door swing closed behind her. She moved more deeply into the room, staring incredulously at the scene before her.

"Chicken pox?" she repeated.

"Yes, chicken pox," he repeated. He shook more corn starch into the water. "You *have* heard of chicken pox, haven't you? Or is that one of those unacceptable diseases that angels with special brooms sweep away from Palm Beach mansions like the plague?"

Lynda gritted her teeth and forced a fake smile. "I've not only heard of it, Mr. Alvarez, I've even had it. I guess my angel was on vacation that season."

Rico looked up from his task. Noting that her own sarcasm was not totally lost on him, she continued. "To the French Riviera, of course."

It may have been a grin, or, just possibly, a smirk. Lynda couldn't be sure. The imperceptible movement of his head didn't tell all that much, but she *felt* a change in his attitude.

That thought in itself was ridiculous. She didn't know him well enough to comfortably sense any of his mood swings, yet she knew the moment his annoyance melted away and was, quite suddenly, inordinately pleased with herself.

Fight fire with fire.

"Can I help?" she asked.

Rico stared at her for the longest moment, then nodded slowly. "If you don't mind getting wet."

"I don't mind."

"Okay. Roll up your sleeves and grab a washcloth," Rico said.

Lynda complied and knelt next to Elena as Rico made the introductions. "This is Mrs. Ortiz's daughter, Elena. Elena, meet Lynda St. Clair."

"Welcome." Elena held out a dripping wet hand, which Lynda promptly shook. "Rico, since Lynda's here to help you, why don't I go upstairs and help Mama with the little ones?"

"Good idea."

Elena rose from her kneeling position and wiped her hands on a nearby towel. "Just give me a holler if you need me again." She walked to the door and turned. "Nice meeting you," she said to Lynda.

"Same here," Lynda said as she began sponging down a little boy. "I'm sure we'll be seeing more of each other." The girl nodded and disappeared into the hallway.

The children in the pool laughed and splashed as both Rico and Lynda worked across from each other.

"Sure of that, are you?" Rico asked.

"Hmm?" Lynda questioned as she sluiced water down the back of a giggling little girl.

"Sure you'll be seeing Elena again, I asked."

Lynda smiled. "Yes, as a matter of fact. I am."

"May I ask the reason behind such confidence?"

"You may. I have the video we made of Home Sweet Home. I'm sure that once you see it, you'll hire me in a minute."

Rico raised his eyebrows. "That good?"

"That good."

"And that's why you're here? To show me the video?"

"And to get you to sign on the dotted line."

"This must be a wonderful video."

"It is. But I'm also a wonderful salesperson."

He stared at her a moment as if trying to determine what was suddenly different about her.

"A multitalented person," he commented, seemingly to himself.

Lynda continued her duties as Rico lifted a little boy onto the rug and wrapped a bath towel around him. He patted him dry gently, so as not to abrade his sores. It was amazing, she thought as she watched him administer to the child. The look on his face was soft, affectionate, almost loving, so contrary to any he had ever directed at her. She'd not thought him capable of such a look.

"Next," he said, and a little red-haired girl lifted her arms to him. "My, my," Rico said with a laugh.

"What is this I have here? Elizabeth Ann? Or a prune?"

The girl giggled and threw her arms around his neck. As Rico turned with the child in his arms, his gaze locked with Lynda's. She watched the expression on his face metamorphose from a silly grin to something else, something deep, dark, delicious.

He held her eyes for the longest moment, and her heart began to pound in her chest. A strange and wonderful feeling accompanied that look, and a warmth that had nothing to do with the tepid water spread throughout her.

Rico broke eye contact. "The water is cooling," he said. "We'd better get them dried off before they get a chill."

They worked together drying and dressing the children in pajamas. Then they scooped out buckets of water to drain the pool to the point where they could pull it out the patio doors and dump it in the backyard.

"Is that it?" Lynda asked, wiping a wet hand across her forehead.

Rico tried not to notice the outline of her lace bra through her thin, saturated, blue blouse. He averted his eyes, but looking at her face wasn't much better. She was flushed with a light sheen of perspiration around her hairline. Her lips were full and pink, and wisps of hair curled at her neck. She was a truly beautiful woman, and as much as he'd like to ignore that fact, his body would have none of it.

His reaction was quick, sharp and powerful. Like a stabbing knife, it was almost painful. He felt himself grow hard, and he wanted to give in to that feeling—

to touch her—but he didn't dare. He turned and dragged the pool back into the den.

"Rico?" Lynda called after him. "I asked if you still need me."

He almost laughed out loud at her innocent words. *Need you? Sweetheart, if you only knew . . .*

Rico set the pool back in the center of the room, then turned toward Lynda. "We have four kids to go. If you have to leave—"

"No, no," Lynda said, and followed him into the room. "But why don't we just do this outside? It would save a lot of work."

"The kids have fevers. It's not good to have them sitting with the hot sun beating down on them. It's cooler in here."

"That makes sense," she said, and picked up the wet towels. "What's next?"

"Next we refill the pool. I'll get the hose," he said, and started back out the patio doors.

Just then the phone in his office began to ring. Rico hesitated.

"Go answer it," Lynda said, and she nudged him away from the door. When she passed him, their bodies touched for the briefest instant. "I can handle this."

It took Rico a long moment to regain control. He headed for the door. *Maybe you can, lady, but can I?*

Lynda sat back in the wooden chair and slouched down, a cup of herb tea balanced on her knee. The children were finally all bathed. A quick glance at the wall clock told her it was five o'clock. She still had plenty of time to go home and change before her dinner meeting with the club committee.

She couldn't believe she'd been here for five hours. The time had flown. In stepping over the threshold of the shelter, it seemed as if she'd stepped into another world. Her clothes were still slightly damp from the endless corn-starch baths she'd administered. Her fingernails were encrusted with calamine lotion, which she'd dabbed on little backs and tummies.

She was tired, yes, but also on a bit of a high. The work today was physical, very different from anything she'd ever done. To say she lived a life of luxury compared to the world at large would be an understatement, she supposed. She'd never been without servants to cater to all her needs. Material needs, that was. She saw only a gaping void where her emotional needs were concerned.

Lynda sipped the tea and thought about the children she'd tended today. Her mind couldn't help wandering back to her own childhood, and that one all-too-familiar scene that never failed to sneak up on her. She no longer remembered if the incident really happened exactly that way or if it was just a compilation of many similar incidents that now formed one firm memory.

She remembered waiting at the door in the big house on the beach on one of many days her parents were scheduled to return from some business or pleasure trip. Like a puppy dog, she thought, standing sentinel by the entrance, waiting for her lord and master. Mother would peck the air near her cheek; Father would ruffle her hair. Then they would promise to make time for her at breakfast so that she could fill them in on the events of the days, weeks or months they had been away.

It never failed, though, that the breakfast meeting she'd anticipated with the energy and enthusiasm only a child can have for such a thing, would be cut short or interrupted by a business phone call, an important meeting, or a social event that couldn't wait.

She knew that her parents tried in their own way to make her happy. But the succession of nannies and myriad servants only served to confuse her as a little girl and isolate her as a young lady.

It was no wonder she'd never thought it odd that her husband, Phillip, had treated her the same way. . . as if she were an afterthought.

"Oh, yes, there you are, Lynda. Dinner tonight? Let me check my book. Oh, no, dear, not tonight. I have a meeting at the club. Let me pencil you in for next week. How's Thursday?"

Lynda swallowed a gulp of cooled tea as her stomach clenched with the memory. Why was she so insignificant to those who were supposed to love her? She always tried to be her parents' perfect daughter, and then the wife and helpmate Phillip claimed he wanted. She'd even pushed aside the idea of having children because he said it would be better for them to wait until his law practice was better established. But that never happened. Not for her, anyway. She'd heard the other day, though, that his new wife was pregnant.

She didn't love Phillip anymore; perhaps she never had. But overhearing that bit of gossip in the ladies' room of the club had cut her to the quick.

"Poor Lynda," she'd heard them say.

Placing the cup of cold tea on the table, she stretched. The muscles on the backs of her legs pulled with the effort. She didn't feel like "Poor Lynda," not since she'd made the decision to take charge. She knew firsthand that one of the most uncomfortable places to be was sitting on a fence. Establishing Events, Inc. was the wisest decision she'd ever made. Now all she felt was good about herself. She looked forward to the next day, the next challenge. Her life meant something, something real, something valuable.

She may not have any children of her own, but there were plenty of children right here who needed her help. She thought of the soul-eyed Tomás and smiled. He was as precious as they came, and she had fallen in love with him already.

"Still here?"

"Oh. Yes." Lynda sat up straight. "I hope you don't mind. I made myself a cup of tea."

Rico lifted the cup. "It's cold. How about another?"

Lynda stood. "Sure. I'll make it."

"Sit. Relax. You've done enough today."

He refilled the teakettle and placed it on the burner. "Tired? he asked.

Lynda nodded. "A little. Is everyone settled in?"

"Yes. I think the worst is over. They should be able to go out by the end of the week."

"You were wonderful with the children," Lynda said softly.

"So were you. Thank you for your help."

"I enjoyed it," she said.

Her face was flushed with the compliment from him. Rico suppressed an urge to lean over and kiss her. She looked as if she wanted to be kissed, and he more than wanted to oblige. Her lips were full, moist, and all he'd have to do was brush his against hers with only the lightest touch.

Just thinking about how she would taste started a rumbling deep in his belly, and he turned away. With his back to her, he filled two mugs with steaming water and dipped the tea bags methodically.

Part of him wanted to throw her out; the other part, take her in his arms and make love with her. It was a dilemma, to be sure, and he didn't, for the life of him, know how to deal with it.

He tried to think analytically, taking into consideration only her assets as a professional fund-raiser. But her other assets kept getting in the way. He knew what he should do, but he also knew that it wasn't what he was going to do.

Lynda didn't question his silence. It seemed appropriate right now with the two of them alone—or as alone as two adults can ever be in a house full of children.

"Sugar?" he asked.

"A half teaspoon, please."

He doctored the tea and brought the mugs to the table. Lynda gingerly sipped the hot liquid. He sat across from her and stared into the mug for a long minute before bringing it to his lips. When he did, their gazes met.

His eyes were deep, dark, almost black, and just as fathomless. She wondered what he was thinking, then was suddenly grateful she didn't know. He made her uncomfortable, self-conscious, nervous. He made her all too aware that he was a man and she, a woman. He made her . . . too many things, all of which she didn't want and was not prepared to be.

"If you're not too tired, I'd like you to take a look at the video. I put in on your desk earlier—"

"I know."

"You do? Did you have a chance to look at it?"

"Yes."

"And . . ."

Rico wrapped his fingers around the mug. "It's good."

"You liked it?"

"Yes."

"So . . . am I hired?"

Rico stood and walked toward the sink. He poured the remaining tea down the drain. He was so quiet for such a long time, Lynda wasn't sure he'd heard her.

"Mr. Alvarez?"

He turned to look at her, and leaned a hip against the counter.

"Rico," he said softly.

"I beg your par—"

"If we're going to work together, you'd better start calling me Rico. Everyone else does."

Lynda's smile was heart-stopping. She stood and walked around the table.

"I have the job?"

"You have the job, Lynda. May I call you Lynda?" She nodded and he continued. "With one condition."

"Anything."

He raised his eyebrows at her quick reply. "Don't you want to know what it is first?"

"I can't think of anything I won't do to work on this fund-raiser," she said honestly.

"That's all well and good. But I want your word that this won't become a three-ring circus. Keep it modest, and keep my and the children's involvement to a minimum."

Lynda was elated. She felt victorious and completely in control for the first time since meeting him. She put out her hand to shake on the deal. He took a step forward and took her hand in his.

Lynda's smile faded. His touch was electric, and that control she was so proud of a moment ago disappeared as quickly as it came. She tried to read his mind through those dark eyes, but too many other things were getting in her way—like the look on his face, the shape of his mouth and the heat in the hand that was gently squeezing hers.

Rico felt her tremble, and it excited him all the more. Now was not the time to pursue exactly what that trembling meant, as much as he'd like to. The best he could do was file it away, and hope he could handle it when and if the right moment ever did present itself.

"You have my word, Rico," Lynda said, conviction in her voice and butterflies in her stomach. "I promise that I won't do anything you don't want me to do."

He studied her face for a long moment. "And I promise you the same."

Lynda looked down at her hand in his. It was a promise she could live with.

Wasn't it?

Four

Lynda allowed the waiter to refill her coffee cup. She added a drop of milk and stirred as she observed the women at the table. They represented her unofficial committee, and she always passed her plans by them before implementation.

In reality, they were the driving force behind any successful fund-raiser. They were the ladies from the club, the movers and shakers of local society who could make or break a program. Without their support, any charity, no matter how worthy, would wither and die on the vine.

She took a sip and glanced at the women over the rim of the cup. Each seemed the pampered wife or daughter of a wealthy businessman. Lynda knew better. Pampered, yes, but in their own way, these women worked hard for what they had. They devoted their lives to making other people's lives run smoothly—

spouses, children and those less fortunate than themselves. They had a strong feeling of obligation to always do the right thing, as if along with their wealth and privilege came a responsibility to give something back.

They were her friends and had supported her during good times in her life and bad. She knew their faults as well as they knew hers, but when push came to shove, they would close ranks and protect each other to the death.

She wondered how Rico would view them. Would he misinterpret their attitudes as snobbery? She thought he would. She couldn't imagine him fitting in here, at the club, with these people. His world was too basic, too involved with the struggles of day-to-day life to understand or relate to what drove women like these—women like her.

"You're getting better and better at this, Lynda," Barbara Johnson said, holding up the papers she had been reading. Her half glasses were perched on the tip of her nose, attached to her neck by a gold chain. She tilted her head upward to get a better look. "I remember the first program you put together. In comparison, this is first-rate. I'm impressed."

"Thanks," Lynda said. "Like anything else, practice makes perfect. I must admit, though, that this project is especially close to my heart. You should see those kids—"

"I'd like to see the man in charge," said Jocelyn Hart, the sultry brunette to Lynda's right. "Mr. Alvarez seems very interesting. When do we get to meet this paragon?"

Lynda felt her stomach lurch. Rico would definitely not want to be involved in a "dog and pony show" for the ladies at the club. "You don't. Mr. Alvarez is too busy with the shelter at the moment. He won't be directly involved in the project."

"That makes no sense," said Meg Palmer from across the table. "If we're going to support Home Sweet Home, we'll need to meet with him. He's the owner/operator of the shelter, isn't he, Lynda?"

"Well, yes—"

"Then, what's the problem?" Meg continued.

"It's his request," Lynda said lamely.

Barbara dropped her glasses from her nose and let them fall to her neck. "You can't expect us to solicit funds for this raffle, dinner and donor book without meeting the man behind it, can you? Lynda, really, that's totally unreasonable."

"I for one cannot ask my husband to donate the car for the raffle unless I've at least had a chance to talk to the man," Meg said. "We've *always* had preliminary meetings with the people involved."

"You've seen the video. What else is necessary?" Lynda said. She was beginning to feel boxed in.

"What is it, Lynda?" Jocelyn leaned closer to her, elbow on table, resting her head on her hand. "Want to keep him all to yourself?"

"Don't be ridiculous!" Lynda said. She was more than aware of Jocelyn's interest in Rico, the man, from the comments made during the screening of the video. Jocelyn was between husbands at the moment, and that always meant trouble for any reasonably attractive male within striking distance. "I hardly know the man. This is business, Jocelyn, and it was his decision not to be involved. In fact, I had to promise him that in order to get the project in the first place."

Jocelyn sat back, Megan sighed and folded her arms, and Barbara slipped the proposal back into its folder.

"I think you'd better talk to him again, Lynda," Barbara said, obviously speaking for the group. "Explain to him that we only want to meet with him. He is, after all, the representative of Home Sweet Home. I'm sure he'll understand our concerns."

"It's a legitimate organization—"

"We're not questioning that. We know you, and your recommendation is good enough for us. But we are talking about an awful lot of money here, Lynda. And a lot of time and effort. I don't think our request is unreasonable, do you?"

"No, of course it isn't. It's just that he's so busy—"

"Why not ask him to lunch? Here, at the club," Jocelyn suggested. "He has to eat lunch, doesn't he? Why not here? It won't cut into his time too much, and we can all have the opportunity to talk to him informally."

"That's a splendid idea," Barbara said.

"Suits me fine," Meg added.

"Then it's settled," Jocelyn said. "How about the week after next?"

All the women nodded and turned to Lynda.

"Okay, okay," she said. "I have to meet with him to go over the plans. I'll ask him then." She sighed. "He'll be here." *I hope.*

Lynda glanced at the clock over the wall oven for the fifth time. She rocked back and forth on the stool as she sat at the kitchen counter toying with the fringe on a colonial blue woven place mat.

"What time are they supposed to be here?"

Dee looked up from her task of shredding lettuce into a large salad bowl. "The same time I told you a minute ago. About six-thirty. Steve is picking Rico up on his way home."

"It's six thirty-five already."

"They'll be here soon."

Lynda stood and walked around the kitchen table, turning a knife, moving a glass, readjusting a napkin as she ambled.

"Will you please sit down and relax!" Dee said. "Have a glass of wine. It's a new Chardonnay from California Steve picked up last night. It's supposed to be very light and dry."

Dee poured the wine into a delicate crystal glass and handed it to Lynda. She took a sip.

"It's good," Lynda said, and peeked out the bay window that overlooked the driveway. "Do you think they hit traffic?"

Dee sighed and dropped the remaining half head of lettuce into the bowl. She picked up a dish towel and wiped her hands.

"Do me a favor, will you? Go upstairs and see if Sarah needs help with her homework."

Lynda turned at the sound of her goddaughter's name. "Isn't she having dinner with us?"

"No, Steve felt this would be a business meeting of sorts between you and Rico, and it would be better if Sarah weren't here to interrupt."

"I wouldn't mind, and I'm sure Rico wouldn't, either," Lynda said. "Sarah's a pleasure. I wouldn't want her to feel left out."

"We asked her, and it was her decision to have dinner early. She has a book report due Friday, and wanted to finish the book tonight. You know how she is," Dee said. "Go on up. You're a nervous wreck! I've never seen you like this before."

Lynda took another sip of wine and stared back at her friend.

"Go!" Dee lifted the wineglass from her hand and gave her a friendly shove.

Lynda nodded and slowly moved from the kitchen through the den to the stairway. Dee was right. She was a nervous wreck. She had spent an inordinate amount of time preparing for tonight's meeting. Steve had suggested they go over the fund-raising schedule informally at his home. Soon Dee got into the act by offering to serve dinner. Suddenly what was supposed to be a business meeting evolved into something else, something almost like . . . a date.

Lynda didn't know what to do. For starters, she hadn't been out on an actual date in quite a while. After she and Phillip divorced, the social whirlwind that had been her life was dramatically reduced. Once she'd become used to spending quiet weekends alone, she'd found she liked it. All her energies were soon directed into her business, and what was left over became cherished personal time she had no desire to share with anyone other than close friends.

Events, Inc. had become the focal point in her life. She loved the work and found she liked being in the driver's seat. Maybe that was the reason for this silly case of the jitters that had overcome her so. All her business meetings were conducted in either her office or her client's. She was comfortable and in control in a formal setting. Somehow the coziness of the Ballingers' kitchen threw her. It was too close, too domestic . . . too intimate.

She'd pondered her fate for a long time, trying to determine why the prospect of sitting across a dinner table from Rico intimidated her so. For the better part of her life she had dealt with a formidable father, then a cool, reserved husband. Mr. Alvarez should be a piece of cake. He was only a man, after all—a man unlike most she knew, perhaps, but still a flesh-and-blood human being of whom she had nothing to fear. The fact that the sight of him gave her butterflies in her stomach had no relevance. She should certainly be able to hold her own with him in a business situation. She had wanted this account, but now that she had it, she wasn't sure she could handle it. Not the work, but the man.

It was his eyes, she decided, that did her in. She had only to gaze into their fathomless black depths to feel as if she were being sucked down into a vortex from which there was no escape. Those eyes haunted her dreams, which were becoming more and more erotically imaginative of late, almost embarrassingly so. In some ridiculous way, she was afraid he would be able to tell what she was thinking just by looking at her.

"Hi, Aunt Lynda."

Lynda looked up. She found herself standing at the doorway of Sarah's room. She shook her head to clear it and smiled broadly at the nine-year-old girl.

"Hi, sweetheart. How's it going?"

"Okay. I'm reading one of the books you gave me for Christmas for this report that's due. I've been saving it special."

Lynda moved into the room and sat down on the twin bed. Lifting the book cover she saw it was one of her favorite classics. She pulled Sarah into her arms and gave her a hug. Sarah reminded Lynda of herself at the same age. Sarah was so serious, and such a planner, that nothing was left to chance. Lynda had been the same way, and in many ways, still was.

For Lynda, being so organized when she was little was a result of her desire to please her parents. She had so craved their praise and attention that she strove to never be a bother to them in any way. She became a very independent young lady, living a life apart from the two adults around whom her world revolved.

Things hadn't changed, either. A number of years ago, her parents had chosen to live in the south of France. They alternated visits, but in many ways their lives had reverted back to the polite, but distant relationship they had always had. Lynda's "family" now consisted of her friends and associates, particularly Steve, Dee, but most of all Sarah, with whom she spent as much time as could be arranged.

She kissed Sarah's head, breathing in her clean, child's scent. In comparison, Sarah was well loved not only by her parents, but by Lynda as well, who had become an adopted aunt at her birth.

"I'm sorry I couldn't make the museum trip with you last Saturday, but I had a gymnastics meet," Sarah said as she returned the hug.

"That's okay. We'll do it some other Saturday. Will that be okay?" Lynda looked down into Sarah's big brown eyes.

Sarah nodded. "If Mom says."

Lynda stroked Sarah's hair. "I'll ask her tonight. We'll have a great day—lunch, ice cream—"

"I think Mom's calling you. Daddy and Rico must be here."

Lynda's hand stilled as she heard voices at the bottom of the stairs, but she didn't move.

"Shouldn't you go down?" Sarah asked.

"Yes. Sure. I'm going." Lynda kissed Sarah's cheek and stood. "Don't forget our date."

She barely heard Sarah's affirmative answer as she made her way out the door and down the curved stairway that overlooked the foyer.

She saw him before he saw her.

Rico was standing beside Steve, an arm resting on the newel post, one foot on the first step. He was dressed casually—jeans, a yellow short-sleeved sport shirt, Dock-Siders, no socks. She stopped midway and stared at his profile for a moment. The gold stud in his left ear caught the light and glinted out at her. His black hair was curled at the collar, still wet from the shower. He was laughing at something Steve said, his face animated.

He was, by far, the most perfect specimen of man she had ever seen.

Steve said something about helping Dee and disappeared into the next room. Rico swung off the post to follow, but stopped dead when he noticed Lynda on the stairs. For a long moment they just stared silently at each other, taking in every minute detail.

Slowly Rico leaned full-length into the post, almost hugging it to him. His lazy gaze roamed over her body, stopping at strategic points before finding her face. Lynda's grip tightened on the oak banister as the heat once again began to bubble in the center of her being.

"Hello," she said softly.

"Hello."

Lynda awkwardly continued her descent until there was only one step between them. As she slid her hand down the banister to the post, she almost touched his arm. Rico didn't move out of her way. They were so close she could feel his warmth. She pulled her hand away and discreetly wiped her damp palm on her slacks.

Lynda cleared her throat. "You're late. Did you hit traffic?" she said conversationally.

Rico shook his head. "No, Steve had to pick up cake for dessert." His eyes never left her face. "You look beautiful tonight."

She did. The words had just slipped out, but they were true. Her golden hair was free, unbound, soft and loose around her face. The skin on her cheeks and nose was pink from the sun, making her eyes appear even bluer than they were, if that were possible. The black slacks were tightly molded to her long legs, and the oversize white top dipped slightly between her breasts.

"Thank you," she said. Lowering her gaze, she took a step around him.

Noting her guarded look, Rico stopped her with a hand on her arm. "I didn't mean to embarrass you. It was a compliment."

"I know." She still didn't look at him.

He had been looking forward to tonight, more than he should have for a simple business meeting. It had been almost a week since he'd seen her. No one was more surprised than he at the excitement he'd felt when Steve had called to make these arrangements. He felt like a kid, all tied up in knots, wondering what to say, what to wear. *Like a stupid little kid.*

The fact that she seemed as cool as a cucumber irritated him to no end.

"It's not too late to change your mind about working on the fund-raiser," he said.

With that, he got her attention. Lynda looked him in the eye. "Why would I want to change my mind?"

"You seem uncertain."

"Not about the work."

"Then about what?" he asked. When she didn't answer right away, he answered for her. "About me?"

"You make me...nervous," she said, a slightly self-mocking look on her face.

"Would it make you feel any better if I told you that you do the same to me?" he asked.

"No. I think it would make me feel much worse."

She placed her hand on top of his and gently picked it off her arm. Rico grabbed hold of her hand before she could pull away. He looked down at it, and gently examined, then caressed each finger before recapturing her gaze.

"Then I'd say we're even," he said softly.

She would swear on a stack of Bibles that those penetrating eyes were capable of swallowing her whole.

Oh, no, not even, she thought. *Not at all even.*

Lynda moved around him and headed for the kitchen, all too aware that he was directly behind her.

"There you are," Steve said as she entered the kitchen. "Visiting Sarah?"

"Yes," Lynda said. "We've made another Saturday date. What weekend is good for you?"

With wet hands, Dee lifted the edge of the wall calendar to check the date. "The fifteenth is fine with me. That'd be a great day for us to go furniture shopping for the den."

Steve groaned at the suggestion as he filled the wineglasses on the dinner table. Dee offered hors d'oeuvres as Steve stepped out onto the deck to grill steaks. The four exchanged small talk. A few times during dinner, Lynda tried to bring up the luncheon at the club next week, but somehow it fell flat every time she opened her mouth.

It was Dee who saved the day.

"Oh, Rico, did Lynda tell you? The ladies at the club want to meet you."

Rico gave a side glance at Lynda, who quickly developed an inordinate interest in her salad. "No, she didn't."

"It's really their modus operandi. They like to check out the people who run the charities. It makes them feel everything is on the up-and-up, you know," Dee said between bites of steak.

"No big deal?" Rico asked.

"No big deal," Dee answered. "Right, Lynda?"

"Right," Lynda said, unbelieving as to how easily Dee handled Rico. Why couldn't *she* do that?

Rico looked at her. "When do they want to meet?"

Stunned at his easy compliance, Lynda took a moment. "Uh, well. Next week? Wednesday? Lunch at the club?"

"Will you be there?" he asked.

"Yes," she said. "Dee, too."

"Fine."

"That was easy," she said, her thoughts becoming words.

"Didn't you think it would be?" he asked.

"No, as a matter of fact, I thought you'd give me a hard time about it. You were so adamant about not being involved."

"Ah, but that was before I *became* involved. Once you get to know me, you'll discover that when I commit to something, I give it my all." His look implied much more than his words.

"I'll remember that," she said.

"Please do."

As Lynda broke eye contact with Rico, she became aware of the silence at the table. Dee and Steve had ceased eating and had been watching their exchange much like a tennis match. She became embarrassed and looked down at her plate, but not before she caught the knowing grin on Dee's face.

When dinner was over and dessert served, Lynda and Rico helped clear the table. In no time at all, they were involved with the plan for the fund-raiser.

Rico paid close attention to Lynda as she laid out the schedule of events. The flyers, invitations to local businesses, raffle tickets all the way down to the detailed menu for the night of the dinner-dance.

He was more than impressed with her program. A new, slightly awed respect for her business acumen began to replace his skepticism. The woman knew what she was doing. He had done some private fund-raising for the shelter in the past, but in comparison to this program, his was amateurish at best.

Her face glowed as she spoke, becoming more passionate as she went along. Her words were important, he knew, and he paid attention to everything she said, but he also couldn't stop himself from falling under the spell of the grace of her movements, the rhythm of her scratchy voice, the scent of her woman's body.

When she reached across the table to open a sample donor book for his inspection, the side of her breast brushed against his shoulder. She hesitated for a moment, then continued with her explanation. Instinctively he reached up and rubbed the spot, as if it burned. And it did. His entire body was on fire with a fierce desire to show her another, more sensual outlet for the passion she displayed.

The night was over too soon for Rico's liking. He could have stayed hours longer if it meant being with Lynda. The thought bothered him. He had no business dreaming impossible dreams, not at his stage of life. Once this fund-raising business was over, he would probably never see her again. It was highly unlikely that they would bump into each other in the future, even at Steve and Dee's. It hadn't happened before, and there was no reason for it to happen now. He'd meant it when he'd said they traveled in different circles.

Better, wiser, smarter to stay clear of her, to keep this *all* business, to keep his resolve strong. It would make the days after less painful. He knew about that kind of pain, and swore early on in life that he'd never subject himself to it again.

Better, wiser, smarter...but the more time he spent with her, the more he was convinced that he was not going to be able to keep his hands off of her indefinitely.

"I'm ready to leave any time you are," Steve said to Rico as he grabbed his keys.

"I told you I should have taken my own car," Rico said. "Now you have to drive back and forth."

Dee came up behind her husband. "I'm sure Lynda wouldn't mind dropping Rico back at the shelter. Would you, Lynda?"

"No, of course not." Lynda said. She knew what her friend was up to, but struggled to keep her expression neutral, even though her heart was pounding at the thought of riding home with Rico.

"It's out of your way," Rico said. "You don't have to—"

"No problem," Lynda said as they took their leave.

They rode in silence until she hit the entrance ramp of the interstate. Lynda tried her best to pay attention to the road, but all her senses were centered on the man sitting near her. At times, she felt his eyes on her, and thought he was about to speak. She held her breath for a long moment, then expelled it when it was apparent he was not.

She was almost calm when she felt him shift in his seat to face her.

"Nice car," he said.

"Thanks. I bought it myself once Events, Inc. showed a profit."

"No gift from Daddy, then?"

Lynda laughed. "No, Daddy stopped giving me gifts like this years ago."

"It suits you," he said.

She gave him a quick, questioning look.

"The car. It reminds me of you." He caressed the leather seat. "Smooth, sleek, classy."

"I don't know if being compared to a car is a compliment, but I'll take it as one."

"Oh, it is. Don't you know that you can tell a lot about a person by the car he or she drives? Don't shake your head. It's true."

"That's nonsense."

"Not nonsense. For example. If I drove a pickup truck, you'd think I was a laborer of some kind who needed it for work. You wouldn't expect me to step out of a pickup in a tuxedo, now would you?"

"No, but—"

"No buts. The same is true about you. I wouldn't expect this elegant Mercedes to be owned by a woman named Naomi with wild, red hair who had a mess of tattoos, one on her upper arm that said 'Hot Mama.'"

Lynda laughed out loud. "Rico, you're crazy. Where did you ever think that one up? Naomi. Really."

"Yeah. Naomi. Really. She lives in Detroit."

"You mean to tell me you actually know someone named Naomi with tattoos?"

"Not only know her. Was—how would you say? 'Emotionally involved' with her for a while. We even have matching hearts somewhere that I won't mention."

"This I've got to hear," she said with a laugh. "When was this?"

"Way back when I was bumming around the country on a Harley."

He became silent for a moment, and suddenly the joking mood disappeared. Lynda sensed he was thinking about something other than those carefree days with Naomi. There was so much about him she didn't know, and she had to admit she had a deep-down hunger to learn all she could.

"Tell me about it," she asked softly.

He shifted in his seat. "Not much to tell."

"Doesn't sound that way. Sounds as if there's a lot to tell."

"Why are you so interested in my life?" he asked.

"Is it so terrible that I'd like to know you better? Maybe if I did, I wouldn't be so nervous around you."

She turned to him, and he saw the look in her eyes. It would be worth a soul's confession to see her relax with him just once.

"Okay. Where do I begin?"

"With Naomi. And the tattoo."

Rico laughed. "Naomi. She was a tough cookie, but sweet, real sweet. I needed someone like Naomi back then." He looked over at Lynda. "I think I'll skip the part about the tattoo."

"How old were you?" she asked.

"About twenty-one, twenty-two, I don't remember exactly. Those years after 'Nam are kind of blurry."

"You were in Vietnam? Fighting?"

Rico shook his head. "No, not fighting. Pushing."

"I don't understand."

He sighed. "You wouldn't. I was with the Marine Evacuation Force. You know, one of those guys that pushed people back from the gates and off the helicopters when we abandoned Saigon."

"I'm sorry," she said.

"Me, too."

"Is that why you became involved with the homeless?"

"No," he said. "I took off after I came home. I couldn't take the idea of going back to school, sitting in a classroom. I needed space, so I bought a motorcycle and just left for parts unknown."

"Just like that?"

"Just like that. My mother went crazy, but I couldn't explain how I felt to anyone. I had to be with people who were as lost as I was."

"Like Naomi."

"She was one. There were others, too. It wasn't a pretty time in my life. But it was a necessary one."

"You came back, though," she said.

"That was years later. And all because of Joe."

"Your brother, the priest."

"Yes. Father Joe now, but always Little Joey to me. He tracked me down. Found me somewhere in California at the time. Said he needed help with this shelter he wanted to start. I wanted to say no, but seeing him standing there with that collar on blew my mind." Rico paused, lost in thoughts of long ago. "Little Joey, a priest."

"So you came back," Lynda prompted as she exited the highway.

"Yes. I came back. We started out in my mother's basement with three kids. Their mother was a junkie who disappeared, and no one knew who the father or fathers of the children were. It mushroomed from there. We had to move out, find a bigger place. Then Joe was assigned to a parish, and I, well, I kind of took over."

Lynda made the last turn onto the street where Home Sweet Home was located. She was sorry the drive was over. There was so much more she wanted to know about him, but now was not the time to ask any more questions.

"We're here," she said softly as she pulled the car onto the pebblestone driveway. She cut the engine and turned off the lights.

"Yes," Rico said. The shelter's front door opened, and two people emerged. "There's Elena and Mike."

"Is that her fiancé?" Lynda asked, knowing from Mrs. Ortiz that Elena planned to marry soon.

"Yes," Rico said. "Elena's staying over tonight to help her mother in the morning. I don't know what we'll do once she and Mike marry. They're planning to move to Tampa."

Rico and Lynda sat in silence and watched as the two young people kissed good-night. Mike leaned against his car and pulled the willing Elena between his legs. The kiss was deep, powerful, mesmerizing.

Lynda felt the confines of the car close in on her as she watched the uninhibited response Elena gave Mike. The girl virtually wrapped herself around his body. Lynda marveled at how comfortable Elena seemed with herself, her body, her love.

She couldn't imagine doing the same herself. Kissing was simple, private, a prelude to making love. Or at least that's what she had always believed. If Phillip kissed her on the mouth, it was a signal that he wanted to have sex. Watching these two made her wonder what she had been missing.

Rico opened the passenger car door. "I think I'd better break this up. Next month's wedding's not coming a moment too soon."

Lynda laughed, and watched the couple break apart as Rico approached. They exchanged pleasantries, and Mike soon left. With a wave to Lynda, Elena went back into the house. Rico walked over to the car, and Lynda restarted the engine. She pressed the button to roll down the window.

The night air was still warm, humid, much as the day had been. Rico leaned over and rested his forearm on the roof of the car as he looked down at her.

"The presentation was top-notch," he said. "You're to be congratulated."

"I'm glad you liked it. I feel good about this program. We're going to make a lot of money for Home Sweet Home."

Rico nodded. "I agree, and we're going to need every cent we can get."

"Oh? Something you care to let me in on?"

"Maybe. I'll let you know."

Rico looked at her for a moment. Then his mouth took hers in a slow, consuming kiss. His lips were warm, full and covered hers completely. She was too stunned to move or react, but neither did she pull away before he did.

Rico stepped back and rolled his eyes to the heavens. "I'm sorry," he said. "I didn't mean for that to happen."

"I-it's all right. Really." She didn't know what else to say. She couldn't think straight.

"Thanks for the ride." He walked backward toward the front door of the shelter.

Lynda nodded, as it seemed the only function she could carry out with any control. He disappeared inside, and she sat for a long moment trying to figure out what happened.

He'd kissed her. That was all, just a simple, thank-you kind of kiss. Gratitude. That was it. Don't read anything more into it, she warned herself.

She rolled up the window and set the air conditioner on full blast. Lynda was feeling somewhat warm and humid herself.

And it didn't have a thing to do with the weather.

Five

It was a perfect day. The sun was hot, bright and high, and the humidity was low. Lynda admired the familiar view as Dee turned her car off the main road by the wood-and-brass country club sign. The curved edge of the Belgian-block driveway was lined with thick Sabal palm trees. The grass was dense, as luxurious as carpeting, and shaved precisely to the nub on the greens. The huge white clubhouse was Georgian, old but well kept.

In many ways, this was a second home to Lynda. Her parents had been members since she was a child and most of her free time was spent on these perfectly manicured grounds. She'd learned to swim here, play tennis and golf. Her earliest introduction to proper table manners had been conducted and reinforced in the dining room.

She was comfortable here; she belonged.

Dee pulled the car into the parking lot made entirely of crushed, sun-bleached seashells. Lynda slid out of the car and followed Dee down the path toward the entranceway. There was activity all around, as tennis players crisscrossed with golfers queuing up to tee off.

Lynda was dressed in a navy-and-white halter and split skirt with complementing navy espadrilles. She and Dee stopped along the way to chat with a few members they knew.

"Are we having lunch indoors or out?" Dee asked as they walked under the coral canvas canopy toward the door.

"Out," Lynda said. "Jocelyn felt it would be more informal."

Dee rolled her eyes. "Jocelyn would."

"Don't start. I know you don't like her, but she's been a real help to me with charity events this year."

"That's because she has so much time on her hands since she's dumped number four. Or is it number five? It's hard to keep up."

"Four," Lynda said. "Promise you'll be good."

Dee made a disparaging sound as she reached for the door handle. Lynda stopped her with a hand on her arm.

"Don't you think we'd better wait for Rico out here? He may not know where to go."

"He's a big boy. He'll find us," Dee said, and she swung the door open.

Lynda hesitated, and Dee turned toward her, holding the door wide for her entrance.

"Really, Lynda. The man is thirty-six years old and has been halfway around the world. I think he'll know how to find his luncheon group by himself. Come on."

Lynda took a quick look over her shoulder before entering the club's main room. The dark-stained oak floors were polished to a high gloss. Formal, antique furniture was arranged on an oriental rug to the right. A reception area was off to the left. Lynda followed as Dee passed down the long hallway toward the back exit to the pool and cabana area.

"Good afternoon, ladies," Maurice, the maître d', greeted them at the entrance.

"We're with Mrs. Johnson's party," Dee said as she and Lynda stood on the brick steps looking over the outdoor tables. "There they are." Dee pointed to a table at the corner of the pool. "We'll seat ourselves, Maurice."

The maître d' bowed and extended an arm for them to pass as Lynda and Dee made their way toward the table.

After greetings were exchanged, Jocelyn looked over Lynda's shoulder. "Well, where is he?" she asked.

Dee took a seat between Lynda and Jocelyn. "Keep your pants on, Jocelyn—and I mean that literally," Dee said. "He'll be here soon."

Lynda suppressed a grin at Jocelyn's pout. The woman was wearing a two-piece, black-and-white, zebra-striped bathing suit with matching skirt. Lynda had to admit she had the body for it, but . . . informal, indeed, she thought as she took a sip of water from the goblet in front of her.

Lynda studied the women assembled and couldn't stop her stomach from rolling over. She was nervous, not for herself, but for Rico. How would he fare with them? she wondered. This was definitely *not* his type.

of place. She would stake her life on the fact that there was not a tattooed body on the premises.

It disturbed her to realize that she wanted them to like him. In a way, she felt as if she were bringing him home to meet the family. She wanted them to approve of him, as if he were something other than what he was, as if he were . . . hers.

It was that kiss, that short, promising kiss he gave her that was causing all this needless worry. It would jump into her mind at odd times of the day, and keep her awake at night. She relived it, over and over again. Short and sweet though it was, she still remembered its power. The problem was, it didn't satisfy her; more to the contrary. What it did was whet her appetite for more. It was a taste . . . just a taste. She couldn't suppress her hankering to indulge herself again—slowly this time so that she could savor every sensation.

They hadn't been together since that night, though they'd talked on the phone. She wondered how she would react when she saw him today.

"Here he comes," Dee said.

Her stomach took an elevator leap. It appeared she would soon find out.

"Good afternoon, ladies."

His voice was rich, deep and welcome. He stood behind her. Lynda could feel his presence, though he was not so much as touching the chair.

Lynda knew all eyes were on the two of them. She expelled a breath she hadn't realized she had been holding and pushed at her chair to stand.

Rico took hold of the back of her chair and pulled it out. He guided her with a hand on her elbow. She was trembling. Was she afraid for him, or of him? Did she fear the man, or only her reaction to him, his touch, the feel of his skin on hers?

She looked over her shoulder. They examined each other for the briefest moment, two pairs of eyes roaming two faces as if starved for the sight of each other. It had been less than a week, she told herself. So why did she feel that nothing short of a month had gone by since she'd seen him?

"Hello," she said, a little breathless. "I'm so glad you could make it."

"Wouldn't miss this for the world," he said for her ears only.

With an imperceptible shake of her head, she warned him to behave. He smiled at her, and her heart skipped a beat. Turning, she made the necessary introductions, seating him in the empty seat to her right.

"Shall we order from the menu? Or pick from the buffet?" Dee asked.

"Let's order from the menu," Jocelyn said. "It will give us more time to talk."

"The buffet is such a waste," Barbara said as she opened the small luncheon menu. "Half the time, no one orders it and the food gets thrown away. It's a shame."

"Someone should complain," Meg said.

"Someone has," Lynda said. All eyes turned to her. "The last time I was here, I asked Maurice to see if he could find an organization to donate the leftover food to each day. You know, some local charity soup kitchen or someplace like that."

When everyone continued to stare at her, but not say anything, Lynda became self-conscious. "Well," she said, as if to justify her actions. "I thought it was a good idea. I saw it on the news. Some hotel restaurants and supermarkets do it. Why not us?''

"No one's criticizing you," Barbara said. "I think it's a wonderful idea. I'm sorry I wasn't the one to think of it."

"What did Maurice say?" Meg asked.

"He said he'd look into it," Lynda answered. "I'll check back with him in a few weeks."

"Getting quite altruistic in your old age, aren't you, Lynda," Jocelyn teased as she sipped her piña colada.

"Perhaps the influence of Home Sweet Home has made Lynda more aware of these things," Rico said softly.

Lynda caught his eye. "Perhaps it has."

His look was as penetrating as usual, but there was something else present. Admiration? She couldn't be sure. She certainly didn't make the arrangements with the club for Rico's approval, but if her self-worth rose a notch or two in his evaluation of her, it was a side benefit she certainly could live with.

The waiter arrived to take their orders, and the conversation turned toward Rico and his work at the shelter. As usual, Barbara jumped in headfirst and took charge, which took the onus off Lynda. She was able to sit back, taking the time to watch Rico as he fielded Barbara's question.

He looked wonderful. He was dressed in a navy blazer, light blue shirt and beige pants. If it wasn't for the earring and his Latin-lover looks, he could pass for a Boston preppie. Had he already owned this outfit, or had he gone out and bought it especially for this occasion? She didn't know, but whatever the case, she appreciated the effort.

"So tell us, Mr. Alvarez," Jocelyn said as the waiter served their luncheon plates. "How did you come to work at Home Sweet Home in the first place? You'll pardon my saying, but you don't look the type."

A slow smile creased Rico's face, and Lynda couldn't help but notice the look that passed between him and Jocelyn. It seemed to her that the two read each other loud and clear. Lynda liked Jocelyn, but knew her to be as toxic as a barracuda when it came to men. From the conversation she had with Rico the other night, it would be accurate to say that Jocelyn would once have been his type. She couldn't help wondering if that was still true.

"I'm definitely not," Rico finally said. "But I was rescued from my evil ways by a man of the cloth."

"His brother, Joe, is a priest," Dee explained. "He's the one who persuaded Rico to get involved with Home Sweet Home."

"I may know your brother," Barbara interjected. "Is he Father Alvarez from St. Bonaventure's?" When Rico nodded, she continued, "I never made the family connection. Wonderful man, and so involved with the community."

"Thank you," Rico said. "I'll mention it to him. I'm sure he'll be glad to know his efforts are appreciated."

"Please do."

Barbara smiled her benevolent smile as coffee and dessert were served, and Lynda knew that Rico had just won her over. By the look on Jocelyn's face, she was thoroughly enamored, which left only Meg.

"Megan," Lynda said. "Don't you have any questions for Mr. Alvarez?"

Meg leaned forward. "Not a question, exactly," she said. "I'm more interested in his opinion. Of all of this," she swept her hand to indicate the country club atmosphere. "Of us."

Rico placed his coffee cup in its saucer and smiled. "Needless to say, Mrs. Palmer, I'm very impressed by your club. The food was delicious, the service impeccable. From what I've seen, everything seems to be beautifully kept and well run." With a charming smile, he looked at each woman at the table in turn. "Which only leads me to the second part of your question. If all of this is any indication of the influence of its membership, I can only hope that the fund-raiser for Home Sweet Home will be so fortunate as to have your support."

Lynda would have shut her mouth if she could, truly she would have. It didn't matter how foolish she looked, anyway, because no one was paying the slightest bit of attention to her. With the conclusion of his little speech, each of the women jumped into the conversation falling all over themselves to assure Rico that he not only had their wholehearted support, he'd have every resource available to them at his disposal.

To say she was flabbergasted would have been an understatement. She was worried about him fitting in? Ha! He worked these women the way a stand-up comic worked the crowd in a nightclub.

While part of her felt vindicated, another, less adult part of her felt annoyed. She was unnecessary. He didn't need her, not for this meeting, and not for raising funds. Hadn't he said he'd been doing all right on his own all this time? Now she could see why. If he took this act on the road, he could open a chain of Home Sweet Homes.

The group dispersed and said their goodbyes, each privately congratulating Lynda with a look or a whispered word. Dee walked over to her, as Megan and Barbara departed, effusive compliments trailing behind them as they made their way to the exit.

Which left only Jocelyn at the table. Jocelyn and Rico.

"It went well," Dee said.

Lynda's stunned look was still apparent on her face. "Went well? I'd say he had them eating out of his hand. And I was worried."

Dee laughed. "I told you he was charming."

"Funny I've never seen any of it."

"You're different," Dee said.

"How am I different? Why was he hostile to me when we first met and not to everyone else?"

Dee shook her head, a wan smile on her face. "If you can't see why, I'm not going to be the one to tell you." She checked her watch. "I told Steve I'd drop in his office before going home. You don't mind, do you?"

"Oh," Lynda said, "I was going to ask you to drop by the shelter. I need to pick up the extra copy of the tape and take it over to the local cable TV station. They're going to view it to decide if they'll run it before the dinner."

"I won't have time to do both before Sarah gets home from school," Dee said. "Why don't you go with Rico, and I'll pick you up on my way back from Steve's office. It'll save time."

Lynda looked over at Rico. He and Jocelyn were sitting close, heads bent, in what appeared to be an intimate conversation. She saw Jocelyn write something out and fold the piece of paper. Rico slipped it into his shirt pocket.

"Maybe Rico's not going right back," Lynda said, more to herself than to Dee.

"Let's ask. I really have to be going," Dee said.

When the two women approached the pair, they broke apart. Jocelyn had a Cheshire cat grin on her face that made Lynda decidedly uncomfortable.

"Lynda needs a lift over to the shelter, Rico. Are you going straight back?"

Rico stood. "Sure. No problem."

Dee kissed Lynda's cheek. "See you later. Bye, Jocelyn." She gave Rico a thumbs-up sign. "Great meeting, *amigo.*"

"Gracias," he said with a smile.

The remaining three stood awkwardly for a moment.

"Well," Rico said to Lynda, "are you ready to go?"

"Yes. Bye, Jocelyn. I'll call you."

"Fine," Jocelyn said. She then extended her hand to Rico. "It was a pleasure, Rico. Perhaps we'll meet again before the dinner."

Rico accepted her hand. "Perhaps we will."

He ushered Lynda out toward the parking lot. The blue Home Sweet Home van was parked at the edge of the parking lot.

"Sorry about the van, but Mrs. Ortiz needed the car today."

"No problem," Lynda said as she climbed in next to him.

She was unusually silent during the ride back. She knew he was expecting her to congratulate him on his fine performance, but for the life of her, she couldn't conjure up the false enthusiasm needed for the task.

Here she had been concerned—almost painfully apprehensive—that he would make a fool out of himself today. As it turned out, she felt like the fool. She'd barely said three words about the fund-raiser during lunch, and then had stood coolly by while he and Jocelyn cozied up to each other. What was on that piece of paper in his shirt pocket? Jocelyn's phone number?

Rico stole a side glance at Lynda, then turned the radio on. She was stewing about something. He had been waiting for her to say something, anything, about the luncheon, but she just sat staring out the passenger window, obviously lost in her own world.

"A penny for your thoughts?" he asked, trying to break through the wall she'd built between them.

Lynda turned at the sound of his voice. She shook her head. "I don't think you'd like to hear them."

"Try me."

"No."

"You're angry."

"Yes."

"Want to tell me why?" he asked. "I thought I handled the ladies very well."

"Oh, you 'handled' them all right. Especially Jocelyn."

"Jealous?"

"Don't be absurd."

"Then, what's the problem? I only did what you told me to do. Answer their questions, be polite and let them look me over. I even dressed up."

"I noticed."

"And . . . ?"

"And you look very nice."

"Thank you."

"You're welcome."

Rico laughed. "So why are you angry?"

Lynda turned in the seat. His profile was to her, and she couldn't help but admire the perfection of it. She wanted to tell him off, but she didn't know how to do it without sounding just what he accused her of—jealous.

"You really didn't need me today, did you? In fact, you don't need me, or Events, Inc. at all. You can play in the big leagues all by yourself, can't you?"

"Is that what's bothering you? The fact that I can hold my own with the swells of society? I told you I've been around. How do you think I've kept the shelter open all these years? I had to learn to cultivate the very same type of people that were at the club today."

"But you don't like it."

"I hate it. But I do it, because it's necessary."

"Is that why you did it today?" she asked. "Because it was necessary?"

Rico looked at her, and she was hit with the full force of his eyes. "No. I did it for you. Because you wanted me to do this. Because it meant something to you. That's why."

Out of necessity, his gaze returned to the road. Lynda didn't answer; she couldn't. She didn't know what to say. She was feeling too much right now. Her emotions were on a white-water raft ride, each taking a different direction. Anger, fear, jealousy...and something else, something she refused to name, or even *think* about was there, too, tangled in the swirl, hidden, and therefore safe...for now.

Rico turned the van down the street of the shelter. It was quiet and free of traffic. He pulled into the driveway and cut the engine.

"Come inside," he said.

He excused himself and checked in. She waited in the hall until he returned. He held open his office door for her, then followed her inside and shut the door behind him. The shelter was quiet. Mrs. Ortiz was out, and an aide was upstairs with the napping toddlers.

Lynda moved to the center of the office and dropped her oversize pocketbook on the chair. She looked around. The video tape she wanted was lying on top of the file cabinet. She picked it up and shoved it into the bag.

"Dee should be here soon," she said, her back to him.

Rico leaned against the desk. "Is that all you wanted?"

It was a mistake to turn. His look was dark, piercing, his body coiled as if ready to strike. There was fire in his eyes. Externally she was cool and collected. Internally the intensity of his look was melting her down. She could kid herself all she wanted, but she couldn't deny what her body was telling her.

Without conscious thought, she moved forward, stopping only a hairbreadth away from him.

"No," she said.

Lynda lifted her hands slowly. She touched him, first tentatively, then fully, splaying both palms flat against his chest. His skin was warm through the soft cotton material of his shirt. She averted her eyes from his face, seemingly fascinated by the movement of her own hands.

Rico stood stone-still. He gripped the edge of the desk so as not to pull her to him. Jaw clenched, he allowed her free rein. She gently massaged him.

He closed his eyes. It was heaven; it was hell. He never wanted it to end.

Lynda continued moving her hands back and forth, up and down, shoving aside the lapels of his jacket for better access. She pressed her palm over his heart and felt its sturdy, steady vibration.

Then she encountered something stiff. She remembered the paper in his pocket, and lifted her hand quickly, as if the spot burned. Reality shattered the illusion, and she moved to pull away from him.

Rico's hands caught hold of her waist and held her in place. "What is it?" he asked.

"Nothing."

He reached up and felt his pocket, then pulled the paper out.

"Is this what's bothering you?" he said, waving the folded paper between two fingers.

"What you and Jocelyn do is none of my business."

"What do you think Jocelyn and I have planned to do?"

"It doesn't concern me." She pulled away.

"Oh, but it does." He took hold of her wrist and pulled her closer. "See for yourself."

Thrusting the paper into her hand, Lynda was forced to look at it. Heart beating with dread, she looked down. It was a check made out to Home Sweet Home. A check, that was all.

She looked up at Rico. He released her wrist. "A donation from Mrs. Hart. And I never refuse a donation."

"I didn't know. I thought—"

"I know what you thought. If you'd asked, I would have told you. Better yet, if you knew me at all you would know that she is not a woman for me."

"But you said, years ago—"

"That was years ago. This is now, today. My tastes have changed. You, most of all, should know that." He rubbed the back of his hand across her cheek. "What is it you want from me, Lynda? Do you know?"

She shook her head. "No."

He confused her so that at this moment she hardly knew what she thought, let alone what she wanted. She only knew that being this close to him excited her beyond anything she'd ever felt for a man before. She wanted to indulge herself, to test herself, her femininity. He'd said someone like Jocelyn was not for him. Did that mean she was?

She looked up at him, able to vocalize the one thing she was sure of. "I only know I want to touch you." Throwing caution to the wind, she moved a step closer to him, and once again raised her hands to his chest. "Will you kiss me? Like last time? Only..."

"Only what?"

"More."

Rico needed no further encouragement. His mind was in overdrive, his body hot and hard. He put his hands around her waist and pulled her between his legs. Their bodies touching, his head descended. He brushed his mouth against hers in a gentle, back-and-forth motion. Their breaths mingled, moistening their lips.

"*Querida,*" he whispered as he slanted his head and captured her mouth in a kiss.

It was a kiss like no other. Her lips parted like the petals of a flower, and he took full advantage of the invitation. His tongue touched hers and mated in imitation of an age-old ritual, thrusting in, out and around, filling her senses, until she could only whimper with need and delight. She could no longer think, only feel.

It was a slow kiss, a long kiss, a hold-your-breath-and-pray kiss. Her heart was pounding, and her hands clenched into the cotton of his shirt, holding on for dear life. She was dizzy, falling, spinning out of control. This was everything she asked for—a kiss ... and more.

They were both breathless when he broke away. Rico leaned his forehead on hers.

"Tell me to stop," he said.

Lynda couldn't speak. Her breath was all but gone, her heart pounding to a staccato rhythm. She looked up at him.

Rico groaned. Her lips were swollen, wet, and to his mind, begging for more. He inched to the edge of the desk as his hands made a slow descent down her spine. He cupped her bottom and pressed her into him.

"Feel me," he said in a harsh, urgent whisper. He nuzzled his face into the crook of her neck. "Stop this, Lynda. Now, or I swear if I kiss you again, we'll make love right here, right now."

It wasn't an idle threat. His body was throbbing, and day or not, office or not, a distinctly primitive side of him said to hell with it all, end the sweet agony, and take her here and now.

Lynda wrapped her arms around his waist. She shut her eyes and hid her face in his chest, losing herself in his warmth, his scent. Her insides were melting into a puddle of want and desire. She could feel every inch of his hard body with the center of all feeling concentrated in the soft cradle of her hips.

She lifted her face and brushed her lips against the skin of his neck, dizzy with the power she had over him.

Rico felt her shy kiss, and closed his eyes as he fought to gain control. He held her close, savoring her softness. A car horn beeped. Somewhere in the back of his consciousness, reason reared its head and prevailed. No matter how much he—they—wanted this, now was not the time.

He shifted. Looking over his shoulder, he noticed Dee's car pulling into the driveway. Rico turned to Lynda and kissed her again, unable to not take advantage of the few remaining moments they had alone. It was a slow kiss, more gentle than before, but oddly enough, just as potent.

He placed his palms on either side of her face, caressing her cheeks with his thumbs. *"Querida,"* he said. "A warning..." His voice was strained with lingering passion and forced control. "If you touch me like this again, I'll take it to mean you want me as much as I want you. Next time, day or night, indoors or out, I won't stop."

With that, he pushed off the desk and released her. Without his support, Lynda's knees gave way, and she splayed her hand on the wall for balance.

"Rico—"

The car horn beeped again. Rico moved to the window and acknowledged Dee's signal.

"You'd better go," he said, his back to her.

She nodded, though he couldn't see her. She was weak, vulnerable and more than a little shaky. Now

was not the time to try to articulate her feelings—even
if she knew what they were. Rico was right. She'd
better go.

With trembling hands, she picked up her bag and
left. He watched her through the window as she
slipped into Dee's car without a backward glance. Like
a scared rabbit, he thought. He knew she had not been
prepared for the force of his passion, or worse, for the
force of her own.

Rico made a vow to himself to leave her alone, to let
her come to him, to let her set the pace. Lord knew if
it were left up to him, there would be no stopping.

Well, he'd warned her. Next time, if there was one,
it was her move.

Next time.

Six

Lynda sat in the kitchen of Home Sweet Home. It was Friday evening, and supper had already been served. Elena was helping her mother prepare the next day's meal. The young girl stood at the sink with the water running, peeling potatoes for boiling. Mrs. Ortiz was close by, frying chicken in two large skillets.

Lynda observed the interplay between mother and daughter. She envied the warmth of Elena's relationship with Mrs. Ortiz. The closest she had ever come to anything like it was with the very same nanny who had given her the porcelain doll when she was about eight years old. The women had been warm, loving and decidedly earthy. Overbearing hugs and kisses had been an integral part of her daily routine. Unused to such attention, Lynda had initially been uncomfortable, but in retrospect, it had been the only time in her life when physical affection was abundantly showered on her.

Her parents hadn't approved of the woman's "familiarity," however, and she was soon let go.

Lynda shook herself out of her reverie when she heard her name. She looked up at Elena.

"Oh, I'm sorry, Elena," she said. "My mind was somewhere else."

"That's okay," Elena said, wiping her hands on a dish towel. "I was asking you if you have plans for two weeks from Saturday."

"No. I can't think of anything off the top of my head."

Elena looked at her mother for encouragement, then apprehensively turned back to Lynda. "Then, Mama, Mike and I would love it if you would come to the wedding. It's nothing real fancy, not like you're used to, but we would be so happy if you would come."

Lynda looked back at the two expectant faces and was basted by the warmth of the two women. "I would be honored to attend your wedding, Elena. Thank you for asking."

As was her nature, Elena bubbled with excitement at the thought of the upcoming event. She lunged forward and hugged Lynda.

"We're going to have the best time!" she said, and grabbed a freshly fried chicken leg. "I can't wait."

"Neither can I," Lynda said.

She couldn't help but laugh along with her. Elena's enthusiasm was contagious. She chatted about the plans for the wedding, the style of her gown and the planned honeymoon in the Bahamas. The more the girl went on, the more Lynda found herself looking forward to the wedding, too, as if she were part of it all, part of the family. As if she belonged.

"*¿Qué pasa?* Why are you hiding there?" Mrs. Ortiz said, looking over Lynda's shoulder. "You should be in bed."

Lynda turned in her chair at the stern tone of Mrs. Ortiz's voice. A contrite-looking Tomás stood in the doorway, his thumb in his mouth.

The children had been put to bed an hour ago. Lynda gave the toddler a mock look of horror, and crooked a finger to him. He smiled and ran to her, climbing onto her lap.

"Horsey," he said.

Lynda grinned at him. She had been teaching him English words, one at a time, but the only one he seemed to remember was "horsey." He pronounced it perfectly and never failed to use it whenever he saw her. He was completely enthralled by the simple ride on her knee.

"All right," Lynda said. "But just one—" she held up one finger "—and then you must go to sleep." She put her hands together and laid her head to rest on them.

Tomás nodded, then held on for dear life as she gave him a vigorous horsey ride.

After the fourth time around, Mrs. Ortiz put her foot down.

"*¡Basta!* Enough!" she said, and lifted the boy away from Lynda.

"It's all right, Mrs. Ortiz," Lynda said.

"He's spoiled," the housekeeper said. "He should be in bed like the others." She started for the stairs.

"I'll take him up," Lynda offered. "You're busy."

Mrs. Ortiz looked at the cluttered countertop and nodded. "*Gracias,*" she said to Lynda. "He's in the second room on the right. Next to Rico's."

Lynda took Tomás's hand and guided him toward the steps. She pressed her index finger to her lips and indicated to him not to make any noise lest he wake the others. Tomás put his finger to his lips in imitation of her gesture and grinned. Lynda couldn't help but smile back at him, even though she knew it was all a game to the mischievous toddler.

Once inside the room, she lifted him into the crib. He stared at her from behind the bars, a sad and forlorn little boy. She kissed his cheek and laid him down, covering him with a light cotton blanket. He yawned, his mouth opened wide, and she smiled. She reached out with her hand to pet his cheek and hair.

He stuck his thumb in his mouth and began to suck vigorously as she caressed him. Within minutes, his eyelids grew heavy, then closed. She continued to touch his baby-soft skin for a few minutes longer, assuring herself that he was truly asleep.

Before leaving the room, she checked the other two cribs and noted that their occupants were dreams ahead of Tomás. She smiled, adjusted the night-light, and left the room.

Lynda noticed the light in Rico's office as she descended the stairs and wondered if he had returned. The mock-up sample of the donor book was completed, and she wanted to show it to him before it went to the printer. She would have come in the morning, but tomorrow was her day with Sarah, and she wouldn't have time.

Preparations for the fund-raiser were right on schedule. The invitations were out, and the money was trickling in at a steady pace from the donor book pledges. Barbara, Jocelyn and Meg were in control of the country club dinner, and the raffle tickets for the

car were selling better than they'd expected. She was
more than pleased with the way things were going.

She couldn't say the same for Rico and her. Since
that fateful day in his office when she all but threw
herself at him, he had not made a personal move in her
direction. He was all business, so much so that at times
she felt as if she were back at square one with him.

But then, what did she want? He'd asked her that
question, and she didn't have an answer. Not then, not
now. She had no idea what she wanted from him long-
term. If they started something—she wouldn't use the
word "affair"—would it continue once this fund-
raiser was over?

Lynda paused on the bottom step and shook her
head. His life was so different from hers. He lived,
breathed, ate and slept this shelter and the children it
housed. She had Events, Inc. and loved what she did.
She also loved her life-style. If truth be told, she wasn't
sure what sacrifices she would be willing to make. The
fact that he hadn't asked her to make any was beside
the point.

She was getting way ahead of herself. They had only
shared a kiss—a highly erotic and passionate kiss, but
still, it wasn't a weekend in the Bahamas, for heav-
en's sake! She was being too analytical, too concerned that all the pegs fit into all the right holes. This
was nothing more than an attraction between two
people from very different backgrounds.

Opposites attract. Didn't everyone say so?

She walked toward the office door, which was half-
opened. She was about to knock when she saw a man
standing behind the desk looking through a folder. He
was dressed in cutoffs and a sweat-dampened T-shirt.

He looked up when she stepped into the room. She recognized him immediately.

"You must be Rico's brother, Joe," she said. "The priest."

Joe looked down at his disheveled appearance. "Does it show?"

Lynda laughed. "No, it doesn't show. I've just heard so much about you."

"Then you must be Lynda," he said. "I've heard a lot about you, too."

From the way he said it, Lynda wondered what he'd heard, and more importantly, where he heard it. In the confessional? She felt the heat rise to her face.

"All good things, I hope," she said.

He grinned, and she noted the resemblance between him and Rico.

"All good things, of course."

He wiped his hand on his cutoffs and extended it to her. They shook. "Sorry about the mess. Rico and I just played some basketball at the schoolyard. If I had known he had company, I'd have taken him up on his offer to shower."

"Not on my account. I'm not company."

"So I've heard. Mrs. Ortiz can't stop bragging about how much you help around here. You'll have to be careful," Joe teased. "If you spend too much time, you'll find you have a permanent position."

"I'm sure Lynda is not interested in such a drastic career change, Joe," Rico said before she could answer.

Lynda turned at the sound of his voice. He was leaning on the doorjamb munching on a piece of chicken. He smiled, and seemed quite at ease. Yet she sensed a restlessness in him. He was about as relaxed as a coiled snake just before a strike.

"Isn't that true, Lynda?" he said.

Lynda opened her mouth to speak, then decided against it. She knew what he was doing. Once again he was testing her, baiting her, and as usual, she had no notion of the answer he expected. She studied him instead, arching her brows and gracing him with her cool look, the one she knew bothered him as much as his sarcasm bothered her.

Rico passed behind her to the file cabinet in the corner of the room. He bit into the chicken, then slowly, laboriously chewed. Mimicking her, he also raised an eyebrow, adding a slight tilt to his head as he awaited her answer. She would have ignored him completely, but felt Joe's curious eyes on her.

When in doubt...she told herself, and opted for the truth.

"Yes," she said finally, turning to address herself to Joe. "Rico's right. I'm very happy with my work. I have no interest in changing what I do. Sorry, Joe."

"You see." Rico picked up the light banter with his brother. He sat on the corner of the desk. "It's not easy to recruit workers for Home Sweet Home. I've been telling you for years."

"You were pretty easy," Joe said with a grin.

"Ah, but you had a formidable ally." Rico reached over and flipped the gold cross hanging on a chain around Joe's neck. "I didn't stand a chance."

"Maybe I'll work another miracle on Lynda," Joe joked.

Rico bowed his head and watched the descent of the chicken bone as he dropped it into the wastebasket. He lifted his eyes with exaggerated nonchalance and looked directly at Lynda. His gaze moved over her face, stopping at each one of her features as he slowly studied her. She felt naked, exposed, and wondered what he was up to.

He turned from her and slapped Joe on the back. "That's exactly what it'll take, *hermano*. A miracle."

Joe laughed. "I don't know about you, but I haven't had any dinner yet. That chicken smells too good to pass up. How about we raid the kitchen?"

Lynda walked behind Rico as they made their way back into the kitchen. Though he confused her, she couldn't deny the pleasure she felt from just being with him. He had a masculine grace that was irresistible. With each time she saw him, it was becoming increasingly more difficult to fight her desire to reach out and touch him.

Tonight was no exception. He was dressed in jeans and a tight-fitting T-shirt. His hair and body were still wet with beads of water from his shower. Being with him, near him, was fast becoming an addiction, one from which she had no wish to be cured.

She moved aside as Joe reached over her and attacked the platter of food. Rico nudged him out of the way and grabbed another piece for himself. Lynda laughed as Mrs. Ortiz rushed forward and slapped first Rico's, then Joe's hands away from the plate.

"Go! Both of you," she ordered. "This is for tomorrow. There won't be enough food for your trip if you keep eating."

Even with her warning to the others, Mrs. Ortiz lifted a piece of chicken and handed it to Lynda on a napkin. She indicated her thanks and took a bite.

"Trip?" Lynda asked, her mouth full.

Take 4 Free Sensations

—*Plus*—

2 Free Gifts with No obligation

Silhouette Sensations are modern stories of love and intrigue, beautifully written to combine sensuality and sensitivity.

To introduce to you this exciting series we'll send you 4 Sensations, a cuddly teddy bear plus a special mystery gift absolutely **FREE** when you complete and return this card.

We're so sure that you'll fall in love with Sensations that we'll also reserve a subscription for you to our Reader Service; which means you could enjoy...

♦ **4 Brand New Sensations** sent direct to you each month (before they're available in the shops).

♦ **Free Postage and Packing** - we pay **all** the extras.

♦ **Free Monthly Newsletter** - packed with horoscopes, author news, competitions (with prizes such as cameras, televisions and microwave ovens) and much more.

♦ **Special Offers** - selected exclusively for our subscribers.

There's no commitment - you may cancel your subscription at any time. Simply complete and return this card **today** to receive your free introductory gifts.

SEE OVERLEAF FOR DETAILS

Reader Service
FREEPOST
P.O. Box 236
Croydon
CR9 9EL

Free Books and Gifts Claim

YES! Please send me, without obligation, 4 free Silhouette
Sensation romances, together with my free teddy and mystery gift.
Please also reserve a Reader Service subscription for me. If I
decide to subscribe, I will receive 4 Sensations each month for just
£7.00 postage and packing free. If I decide not to subscribe I shall
write to you within 10 days. The free books and gifts will be mine
to keep in anycase. I understand that I am under no obligation - I
may cancel or suspend my subscription at any time simply by
writing to you. I am over 18 years of age.

7S2SS

Ms/Mrs/Miss/Mr _____

Address _____

_____ Postcode _____

Signature _____

"Didn't Rico tell you?" Joe said. "We're going up to the farm."

"Joe . . ." Rico warned between bites.

"What farm?" Lynda asked.

"Is it a secret?" Joe asked Rico. "I didn't know."

Rico sighed. "No. It's not a secret."

"What farm?" Lynda asked again.

Rico wiped his hand on a napkin. "An abandoned citrus farm up near the Indian River. It was a small-time operation that went belly-up a few years ago."

"Why are you interested in a citrus farm? Are you thinking about going into the business?

Rico shook his head. "No."

Realization hit her square between the eyes. "The shelter! You're thinking of moving Home Sweet Home up there. That's what you need all this money for."

"I'm surprised Rico never told you," Joe said, glancing from Lynda to his brother and back again. "His plan from the beginning was to raise enough money to close this place down and open another, bigger place up there. That is, if he doesn't lose his license before then."

"Enough, Joe," Rico said quietly.

Lynda could tell Rico was annoyed at his brother's glibness. It hurt that he hadn't told her, hadn't trusted her. Well, what did she expect? She could kid herself all she wanted, but the fact remained that she wasn't really part of his "family," she was an outsider, a worker hired to do a job, that was all.

"Well," she said, swallowing the lump in her throat. "It sounds wonderful. I wish you luck with it."

Rico saw the hurt on her face. He could kill Joe for bringing up the matter of the farm. He'd intended to tell her, but in his own way, in his own time. Now it was out in the open, and she thought he was shutting her out.

He had been unduly hard on her tonight, the result of his own confusion about his feelings for her. He wasn't being fair, and he knew it. It wasn't her fault that he couldn't control this mad attraction for her, and he had no right to take it out on her. *Grow up, Rico.*

"What are you doing tomorrow?" Rico asked Lynda.

"What? Oh, tomorrow I'm taking Sarah for the day. Remember? Steve and Dee are going furniture shopping."

"Come with us. Bring Sarah along. I'd like you to see the place."

"Rico," Lynda said. "You don't have to—"

"I know I don't. I want you to come. I want you to see what you're doing all this work for. Please."

It was the "please" that did it. He rarely, if ever, used the word with her. That, together with the look on his face.

She refused to mention the fact that, addicted as she was, the prospect of spending an entire day with Rico was more than she could resist.

The day had been damp and overcast when they'd started out, but now glimmers of sunshine were filtering through the cloud cover. Rico glanced into the van's rearview mirror. Lynda had spent most of the ride trying to keep Sarah and Tomás amused. The toddler has been a last-minute addition when he'd wriggled out of Mrs. Ortiz's grasp and climbed into the van after Lynda. Rico had relented and agreed to

take the rambunctious boy along, much to Mrs. Ortiz's relief.

Joe sat in the passenger seat calling out directions
from the main highway down one of many dirt roads
they needed to take to get to the farm.

Now that he'd invited Lynda along, Rico had second thoughts. What would she think of the place?
There was a good possibility she'd think him a fool. It
had been several months since he'd seen it, and even
at that time, it had been a mess. If anything, it would
be in worse condition now.

It wasn't long before he proved himself right. The
sign with the name of the farm was long gone, with
only a rusty chain hanging from the post at the entrance. The driveway was overgrown with weeds and
brush, all but hiding the stones underneath.

The van bounced in one rut and out of another as
Rico slowly drove to the main building, which had
served as the farmer's house. He cut the engine.

"Here we are," he said.

Joe opened the van door, and each of the passen-
gers stepped gingerly down onto the damp, dirt-
packed driveway. Tomás immediately ran up the porch
steps of the house.

"Tomás," Lynda called. The toddler never broke
stride. "Sarah, do me a favor and keep an eye on him.
I don't want him to hurt himself."

"I will, Aunt Lynda. Don't worry. I'll be a good
baby-sitter."

Lynda smiled as Sarah ran up the steps after Tomás
and took him by the hand.

It was hot and humid. Lynda's beige shorts were
stuck to her skin and her blouse plastered to her back.

She picked at her clothing in an attempt to capture any stray breeze and allow it to circulate.

Rico walked around the van to where Lynda and Joe stood. "You okay?" he asked.

Lynda nodded. Joe began to unpack the cooler and food baskets from the van. He glanced over her shoulder at a car coming up behind them.

"Who can this be?" Joe asked.

"It's probably the realtor," Rico said. "I asked him to meet us here. I wanted to walk the place with him."

Rico greeted the real-estate agent and introduced him to Joe and Lynda before the two men walked off together.

"Well," Joe said. "I guess that leaves us to explore on our own." He lifted the baskets in one hand and held out the other for her. "Shall we?"

Lynda grabbed the handle of the cooler and took hold of Joe. He helped her walk around the various ruts and puddles. The sun was out in full force now, and a mist was forming on the ground as the water evaporated. Joe and Lynda left the food in a shady spot by the fence and took Tomás and Sarah for a walk around the grounds.

Next door to the main structure was what looked like a barn of some kind. Inside were some stalls, a tack room and a hayloft. The barn was small, but would be serviceable with work. However, Lynda wondered what on earth Rico planned to do with a barn.

This entire project mystified her. There were so many available buildings down in their area of the state because of the slow real-estate market. It didn't make any sense to her why he would want to move

Home Sweet Home a hundred miles away from everything . . . from her.

That was what was really at the crux of her fear. If this worked out for him and he moved the shelter, when, if ever, would she see him again? Sure, she could work on a yearly fund-raiser with him, but how practical would that be to see him for a few weeks every year? Would that be enough for her? Was that what she wanted?

That damned question again, she thought. *What do you want from me, Lynda?*

"The place has a lot of potential," Joe said.

They were leaning against a battered wooden fence behind the house. A large live oak tree sat back fifty yards or so. It had spreading limbs with Spanish moss hanging down inside. One wide branch held a rope and old tire swing. Sarah discovered it and ran right over to try it out. It wasn't long until Tomás followed, and Sarah had to give up her seat to the little boy. True to her word, she was a good baby-sitter, pushing Tomás with endless patience.

"Yes," Lynda answered. "It's certainly big enough, and there's plenty of property."

"Twenty-eight acres," Joe said. "Rico always talked about something like this. 'Big enough to grow,' he'd say. This is certainly the place for him."

"He could build a town here," Lynda joked.

When Joe nodded, the look in his eyes told her she wasn't far off the mark with her flippant comment.

"Is that what he wants to do? Build a town?"

"Not a town exactly, but a center. A place for the homeless, somewhere for them to call home."

"I had no idea," she said softly, awed by the enormity of such an undertaking.

"Though he doesn't like to admit it, the idea started long ago. He always tells everyone I dragged him back here and conned him into starting the shelter, but it's not true," Joe said.

"Then you didn't find him in California after he came home from Vietnam?"

"He told you about that?" Joe asked. "He doesn't tell people he was in 'Nam. I'm surprised. What did he say about it?"

"He said he wasn't fighting there, he was pushing," she answered.

"If he told you that much, then you should be able to understand all this," Joe said, sweeping his hand around the area. "In my opinion, that's when all this started. He never wanted to see people pushed away, or put in a position where they had nowhere to go. Home Sweet Home was the beginning of that dream. This place, if it works out for him, is the fulfillment."

Lynda looked at Joe and knew he spoke the truth. To say that the truth shocked her would be inadequate. She was numb. She hadn't any idea—none— that he'd ever planned anything as grand as this. No wonder he said he needed "a lot" of money. No wonder he agreed to her fund-raiser, even against his initial reluctance. He would use anything and anyone to reach a goal of this magnitude. Even her.

Lynda turned to Joe. "Why are you telling me all this?"

Joe leaned forward on the fence, arms resting at the elbows. "Because I see the expression on your face, and his, when you look at each other. Because I see something going on between you that is more than business." He turned to Lynda. "Because I think this is something you should know."

Lynda nodded slowly, a thousand feelings contained in the movement, the most important of which was her thanks. She did need to know this. As rattled and overloaded as her mind was right now, she could appreciate Joe's concern about his brother, about her. It was his business to watch and observe people, to give advice, to guide, and she truly appreciated it.

"I'm hungry." Sarah ran up to them with Tomás in tow. "When can we have lunch?"

"Right now," Joe said, and reached down to pick up the two food baskets Mrs. Ortiz had packed. "Let's set up the picnic blanket under that big tree. Last one there is a rotten egg!"

Sarah giggled with glee and ran after Joe. Tomás followed enthusiastically, even though Lynda knew he didn't understand what the game was all about.

Lynda picked up the remaining cooler and followed the three at a more leisurely pace.

They had just set out the food when they noticed the realtor's car depart. Rico soon joined them. He sat on the edge of the blanket and accepted a can of cold soda from Lynda. He snapped open the top and took a long sip. Then he looked at Lynda.

"So, what do you think?" he asked her.

"I think I'm a little overwhelmed. The place is a lot bigger than I thought."

"It needs work," he said.

"For what you have in mind, I'd say you'd be better off knocking it all down and starting from scratch."

He looked from Lynda to Joe, who was suddenly very interested in cutting up Tomás's food. Rico stood and held out his hand to Lynda. She gave him a questioning look, but obliged and allowed him to pull her up.

"Excuse us for a few minutes, will you, Joe?"

"Don't rush on my account. But I can't guarantee there'll be any food left. These are hungry critters I have here." The children giggled as he poked each in the stomach.

"We won't be long," Rico said.

He led Lynda away from the tree, around the barn, to the old house. They walked in silence up the porch steps until Rico stopped in front of the door. He swung the screen open and indicated to Lynda to go inside. He followed, then led the way into the large kitchen.

A smell of mildew assailed her as she took a deep breath and looked around. It was a bright room with double windows over the sink letting in the afternoon sun. There was a gaping hole in the alcove where a refrigerator once stood, but the oversize electric stove and oven still remained in the corner flush against the wall. A battered white table stood in the center of the room, but no chairs surrounded it.

Lynda pushed herself up onto the table to sit. Her bare legs swung in the air as she looked expectantly at Rico.

"What did Joe tell you?" Rico asked.

Lynda shifted and leaned her weight back onto her palms. "Your plans for the place. I had no idea, Rico."

Rico nodded slowly. "Crazy, huh?"

She shook her head. "No, not crazy at all. I'd call it wonderful." She meant it, so much so that she had to fight the tears that threatened at the backs of her eyes. She was so proud of him, she had an ache in her heart.

"I always thought," he said, "if you were going to dream, dream big." He looked around at the dilapidated room. "This is one hell of a big dream, wouldn't you say?"

"I'd say if anyone can do it, you can."

"So, you think it's possible?"

"With money. Lots of money."

"The fund-raiser—your fund-raiser—will be the start," he said.

"Yes. A big start. What did the realtor say?" Rico gave her a price. "That's reasonable," she said.

"I thought so, too."

"Then you're going to do it?" she asked. "Buy the farm?"

He laughed at what could possibly be the double meaning of her phrase. "Yeah. I'm going to buy the farm." He reached over and stroked her face with the palm of his hand. "Thank you for coming today. I'm glad you're here."

She leaned into his hand, closing her eyes at the sensation of his skin touching hers. "I'm glad, too," she whispered.

Rico captured her face in his hands. Lynda put her arms around his waist and leaned into him. He kissed her, slanting his mouth over hers and masterfully taking all that she was offering. His tongue swept through her mouth and touched hers, tasting her special, sweet flavor of woman.

He moved his hands from her face, down her arms, to her waist, then lower, to the tops of her thighs. He grabbed hold of her under the knees and pulled her to the edge of the table. Pushing her legs apart, he drew his body into the cradle of her hips.

Lynda felt his heat pressed up against her as his lips left her mouth open and wet, wanting more. He rained kisses on her chin, throat, neck, around to that soft spot behind her ear, where he whispered Spanish words she didn't understand. She didn't have to. The movements of his body told her exactly what he meant.

She clung to the back of his shirt, bunching the material in her fists. An ache grew in her belly, a need so strong, so powerful, she was unable to compare it with any sensation she had ever felt or experienced.

This was want. This was desire. This was what all the writers wrote about, what all the singers sang about. She was dizzy, breathless, hungry, anxious, hot and ready for all he had to give her.

When his hand reached up and unfastened her blouse, she let him. He pushed aside the material and splayed both palms against her midriff, thumbs meeting in the center. For a moment he didn't move. Lynda closed her eyes. His touch was warm and dry, but that didn't stop the chills from running down her back.

Hesitantly, as if he expected her to stop him at any moment, Rico reached around and unsnapped her bra. The scrap of lace fell forward with the weight of her breasts. He cupped one in each hand, first caressing, then massaging the pink buds of her nipples with his thumbs.

Lynda sucked in her breath at the tingling sensations that shot through her. She opened her eyes to follow his dark, passionate gaze. She watched as he gently pinched each tip into pebble hardness. The sight of his tanned skin against her white flesh was mes-

merizing. She whimpered as tiny jolts of pleasure ric-
ocheted inside her in tandem with each movement of
his hands.

His fingers continued their assault as his lips returned to hers. She opened her mouth for him, bit-
ing, licking, sucking on his lips with wild abandon.
She had never been this hot, this needy, in her entire
life. She wanted to drag him down onto the table and
make love with him here and now.

It was Rico who pulled away. With unsteady hands,
he reached behind her to reattach her bra. She looked
up at him questioningly. He cocked his head toward
the window, and she suddenly became aware of the
sound of voices outside. His eyes were heavy-lidded,
glazed with the fire of his need.

"Soon," he said, his voice unusually harsh and
strained. "We will finish this." He moved into her and
she felt the strength of his arousal. "I want to be
here," he pushed into her again. "Right here, inside
you. Tell me you want the same. Tell me, *querida*."

"Yes," she said, barely able to breathe, let alone
speak.

Rico backed away from her as the sound of foot-
steps grew louder. His black eyes looked deeply into
hers, and she saw the determination, the promise. She
reached up and rebuttoned her blouse, her eyes never
leaving his.

He nodded slowly. "Soon."

Seven

Lynda checked the rearview mirror before running the yellow caution light. She was late. As she jumped the speed bump in the church parking lot, she heard the organ music drift from the opened door. She cut the engine, grabbed her purse and hurried along the stone path. A light breeze caught hold of the wide brim of her yellow voile hat, and she secured it with the palm of her hand. She sneaked into the side entrance in hopes that she hadn't missed the bride.

Slipping into the back pew, she noticed that the bridal party had already made their way down the white runner and were standing at the altar. She stood on her tiptoes to see if she could catch a glimpse of Rico, but the crowd obscured her vision.

She did see Joe, however, resplendent in his white and gold vestments. He stood on the altar steps smiling serenely, looking infinitely more pious than the last time she'd seen him with a child on his knee and a chicken leg in his mouth.

The maid of honor passed unescorted, her gown vivid pink and off-the-shoulder. Once the girl climbed the steps to the altar, all eyes turned toward the entranceway as strains of the wedding march announced the main arrival.

Elena was the quintessential bride. Her long black hair was pulled back with curls cascading behind. The headpiece of fresh flowers framed her oval face. Her gown was dusted with seeded pearls on a lace background. The neckline was scooped, and long, tight-fitting lace sleeves ended in points on the backs of her hands. Her tiny waist accentuated the full skirt and five-foot-long train that trailed behind her. She held her head high and her bouquet in her left hand.

Her right was slipped through the arm of a man who looked remarkably like an older, male version of Mrs. Ortiz. Lynda assumed this was the Uncle Ramon about whom Elena always spoke. She knew Mrs. Ortiz was a widow and that she had two other children, a son and a daughter, both older than Elena, and both married with children. The man's face beamed with pride as he escorted Elena toward the altar. She watched as he handed Elena over to Mike and stepped back to slip into the first pew next to Mrs. Ortiz.

Joe began the ceremony with a message about the importance of marriage. As Lynda listened to his words, she felt the tears well in her eyes at their beauty and meaning. She recalled her own wedding to Phillip, and the cold, antiseptic civil ceremony in the office of the local justice of the peace. Her parents had been away, as usual, and Phillip had talked her into a quick, simple ceremony. It had all made such sense at the time, but somehow she always felt as if she'd been cheated of something very special in her life.

Mike and Elena exchanged the vows they had written themselves, pledging their love to each other in their own words. As happy as she was for the young couple, Lynda couldn't stop a hollow ache from taking hold in her stomach. This was the kind of love that she had always dreamed of, but never knew firsthand.

Phillip had said he loved her, but had never shown it. She was ignorant of this visible side of love: touching, sharing, caring, commitment. Sometimes she wondered if she ever would experience such a love. Sometimes she wondered if she were even capable of doing so.

She wanted to—oh, how she wanted to—but her fears of inadequacy were strong. It would take a very special man to make her feel secure enough to even try. Someone who could set her mind as well as her body on fire. Someone who could see into her soul, and know the depth of her hidden passion.

Someone...

Lynda spotted him in the second row as she leaned out into the aisle to get a better view of the bride and groom sealing their vows with a kiss. At the same moment, Rico turned his head and their eyes met. A cheer went up in the crowd, but she was oblivious to the sound.

Their gazes locked, and a glorious warmth seeped into that hollow spot in the pit of her stomach. A wave of emotion crashed over her and spread through her body at the promise in his eyes. She wanted to leave her space and walk to him, wrap her arms around him, and steal his heat.

She smiled at him, and he nodded his head in reply. As the ceremony concluded, Elena and Mike rushed down the aisle out toward the vestibule. Elena's eyes widened with pleasure as she spotted Lynda, and Lynda waved as she passed. It took an inordinately long time for the church to empty as each guest paused to wish the couple well.

Rico indicated to Lynda that he would wait for her outside, and she perused the crowd from the top step once she'd made her way through the receiving line.

He was standing by a limousine talking to some people as she approached. He excused himself and met her on the church steps.

"Hello," he said as he took her hand. "I didn't think you'd make the service."

"I was late and had to sneak into the back. But I did see Elena come down the aisle. She looks so beautiful."

"Yeah. All grown-up. Makes me feel old."

He didn't look old. In fact, he looked fabulous. The navy-blue suit almost made him seem like a conservative banker. Almost. His black hair and brooding good looks gave him too much of an air of mystery. And then, of course, there was the ever-present earring, which disproved any possible connection to the Establishment.

Rico took her hand and led her away from the crowd.

"Where's your car?" he asked.

"In the back of the lot." She pointed around the church. "Do you need a ride to the reception?"

"If you don't mind company."

"Not at all," she said, dangling the keys in front of him. "You can drive."

Rico took hold of the key ring and remembered another time a blond socialite tossed him her keys. A flash of that long, sleek, red Cadillac streaked through his mind. He looked up. Lynda's face was so full of innocence, so void of malice, he dismissed the comparison completely.

"Come on." He guided her through the crowd toward the parking lot.

Lynda filled Rico in on the status of the fund-raiser during the ride from the church to the reception. She hadn't seen much of him this past week, as she had been unusually busy. The dinner-dance was only weeks away, and all the last-minute things that could go wrong were going wrong.

The printer couldn't finish the donor book on time—or so he claimed, until she'd found someone else to do the job. Then, the man just happened to have a cancellation and decided he could accommodate them. The fact that she would never use him again didn't make all the aggravation any easier to deal with.

In addition to the printer, the menu had to be changed. The caterer couldn't get the artichokes for the appetizer of lobster tarragon on artichoke bottoms, so a new appetizer had to be picked from the list. Which meant that Barbara had to have a meeting with the rest of the committee to decide. She loved Barbara, she truly did, but sometimes her autocratic ways made life more difficult than it had to be.

Rico listened as she vented her frustration, but he was barely aware of what she said. He kept glancing at her, more than the conversation warranted. Each time he saw her, she was more beautiful, and today was no exception. She was tempting in her bright yellow outfit—like some sort of decadent lemon confection. She made his mouth water. He knew she had no idea how her appearance affected him; she was so unselfconscious of her looks.

His entire body was wired to the hilt in anticipation of this evening, much more so than his mind. His rational side knew that any further involvement with Lynda was a mistake. He had too much to do with the work he'd chosen to expend energy on a lost cause. But his body wasn't listening to a word he said. His libido was dancing to the beat of a different drum, one with a rhythm and purpose all its own. His blood was pounding through his veins as thoughts of making love with her swirled through his mind.

He'd told her he wanted her. In truth, it was beyond want, beyond need. He ached for her, throbbed for her, was on fire for her. He'd pictured her in bed with him a thousand times. Reaching for him. Touching him. Naked. Beneath him—

"Are you sure that's what you want, Rico?"

He went blank. She couldn't have read his mind, yet he had no idea what she was asking. "Sure," he said, hoping it was an acceptable answer.

"Then I'll tell Barbara to go ahead with the changes?"

"Whatever you say."

Lynda gave him a puzzled glance. He was acting very peculiarly. She hadn't the faintest idea what he was thinking. She'd tried to keep the conversation impersonal, despite her own strong wish to pick up where they'd left off that weekend at the farm. But it seemed not to be. Rico was remote, distant. She wondered if he even remembered what he'd said to her.

Soon.

He turned the car into the South Beach area, an old section of Miami that had recently become the new "in" spot of the trendy crowd. The reception was being held in a small, refurbished art deco hotel nestled along the palm trees of Ocean Drive. Half of Mrs. Ortiz's relatives worked in the hotel in various capacities, which enabled the housekeeper to afford to give Elena a night she would always remember.

Other guests were arriving at the same time, and they had to wait on line for the valet. Once inside, they were greeted at the door by a young man and woman who pinned boutonnieres to each of them. It was a small gold wedding ring intertwined through a bit of white tulle lace. A white ribbon printed in gold with the name of the bride, groom and the wedding date tied everything together.

"It's a custom," Rico explained. Lynda adjusted the favor on her bolero jacket. "A remembrance."

Rico took her hand and led her inside the large room, which was soon filled with people. A waiter wove through the crowd with a tray of hors d'oeuvres.

"Try one," Rico said. "It's *pastellos.*"

Lynda bit into the tiny turnover. "Tastes something like a cheese puff."

"Close enough," Rico said.

They headed toward the bar that was set up in the corner. Lynda sipped white wine as Rico introduced her to Mrs. Ortiz's myriad relatives. Being an only child born of two parents who were only children themselves, Lynda soon became lost in the crowd of uncles, aunts, cousins, nephews and nieces that was paraded before her. By the time the bride and groom appeared, she was thankful for the reprieve, convinced of the fact that she'd never be able to connect more than a few of the faces and names.

The celebration was very family oriented. After the groom, Elena danced with her uncle, brothers and every male relative present. Lynda spotted Debbie Marshall, the nursery school teacher from Home Sweet Home, and the two women struck up a conversation. Rico excused himself, and Lynda lost him to the crowd as one group after another pulled him into their ranks.

She relished the opportunity to observe him in these surroundings. This was his culture, his element. It gave her insight into a lighter side of him she'd never seen. Though she had been amazed at how well he'd fit in with her country club cronies during lunch that day, she was just as awed now by the camaraderie she witnessed as he bantered back and forth in Spanish with the men around him. He was truly an enigma, as at home here in his world as he was in her more reserved one.

When Rico returned to her, he caught her by surprise. Lynda turned as he tapped her on the shoulder and led her onto the dance floor. His jacket was off, his tie loosened, and his black hair fell onto his forehead. He was in a playful mood, and it was contagious. The band was playing a fast, old-style lindy, and Rico twirled her around the floor. Lynda laughed out loud at his antics, her heart thumping to the beat of the music as well as the excitement of being in his arms.

When the music ended, they walked off the dance floor arm in arm. The room was warm, and Lynda shrugged out of her jacket. The dress beneath had a halter neckline, and she fanned her bare skin with the back of her hand. Rico helped her remove the jacket, placing it on the back of her chair. He lingered behind her for a long moment, and she felt his breath on her bare back.

She looked at him over her shoulder, and their gazes locked.

"Warm?" he asked.

"A little."

Gently he shifted her hair to the side and blew cool air on her heated skin. Chills spread like wildfire down her spine, and she instinctively leaned back into him.

As much as he wanted her, he was unprepared for the powerful jolt of desire that shot through him. He knew this evening was going to be difficult for him to control, but this was ridiculous. He'd barely touched her, and already his body was rock hard and ready for more.

He stepped back. Mindful of their audience, Rico caught hold of her shoulders and sat her down before seating himself in the chair next to her.

Lynda stared at him with dreamy eyes. She reached up and pushed back the tendril of hair that had fallen onto his forehead, running her fingers through his hair more than once to keep it in place. For moments too long to measure, they continued to look into each other's eyes, lost to the sights and sounds around them.

The music stopped, and the master of ceremonies announced that dinner was being served, and people began to line up at the buffet table on the opposite side of the room.

"Shall we get something to eat?" Lynda asked.

Rico nodded, though food was the last thing on his mind. He did accompany her to the table and point out certain dishes that she should try.

Lynda had never seen so much food in one place in her entire life. A roast suckling pig held the central place of honor on the banquet table, surrounded by an appealing array of vegetables and salads. Rico made suggestions of some traditional dishes for her to try. He plopped a spoonful of what looked like potatoes on her plate.

"Try it," he said. "It's yucca. A root. It's made with garlic, onion, olive oil." He lifted a morsel to her lips and she tasted it. "Delicious, no?"

"Delicious, yes," she said. "Also fattening."

Rico grinned. "Let it go. It's a wedding. Indulge yourself."

Impulsively Lynda leaned forward and gently brushed her lips against his. "Oh, I fully intend to." Turning her back to him, she continued down the line.

Rico stood stock-still, incapable of movement. Someone nudged him to move on, and he did, following her to the table. He caught her watching him at odd times during the meal. There was a question in her eyes, or an answer, he couldn't be sure which. All he did know was that when she looked at him like that, the food in his mouth tasted like sawdust.

Rico put down his fork and pushed the plate away. It was useless to pretend. The only thing he wanted to taste tonight was Lynda. Without excusing himself, he lifted his jacket off the back of the chair and left the table. He needed to get away from her, from the room. He needed air and time to think.

The party moved into high gear as all the traditions were followed. Elena and Mike fed each other cake.

The garter was thrown and fought over by overzealous young men in the group, and the bride tossed her bouquet. Joe caught it by accident, which set the crowd to roaring.

Lynda searched the room for Rico as she ate the dessert of wedding cake and flan, but he was nowhere to be found. She paid less attention to her conversation with Debbie, as she kept one eye on the doorway.

Soon after, the bride and groom took their leave, though the reception was still going strong. The crowd was loosening up even more than before, holding hands, dancing in circles to traditional wedding songs. Elena's sister came forward and tried to persuade Lynda and Debbie to join in. Lynda shook her head, but Debbie was virtually pulled out onto the dance floor. Lynda laughed and clapped along to the beat of the music as she watched from the sidelines.

As she turned toward the doorway this time, her gaze locked with Rico's. Apart from the crowd, he leaned against the wall. His face was serious, contemplative, so much so that she wondered if something was wrong.

Lynda made her way toward him as the dancing came to an end. She had to weave through the exhausted dancers who fanned themselves as they returned to their tables. The band changed the pace and began to play a slow love song. Rico came forward and met her halfway. Taking hold of her hand, he led her onto the dance floor.

He wrapped his arms around her and pulled her close. She leaned into his body and did the same. Resting her head on his chest, she closed her eyes to listen to the rhythm of his heartbeat. The song was a Spanish ballad, filled with poignant pauses. The sultry melody suited her mood as it soothed and aroused her at the same time.

Rico was barely moving. Lynda looked up into his eyes. It was remarkable how she was now able to read him like a book. The look that once intimidated no longer had the power. She could see beneath his facade of indifference. He seemed troubled, confused, and she felt as if he wanted to say something, but didn't know how.

"What is it?" she asked.

Without a word, Rico took hold of her hand and kissed the tips of her fingers. He threaded his fingers through hers and pushed her hand into his jacket pocket before releasing his grip. She felt her way around the object nestled within, and pulled out a piece of plastic. At first she thought it was a credit card, then realized what it was. An entry key to a hotel room. So that's where he'd disappeared to! Rico had booked a room in the hotel. She held the card in her hand and looked down at it.

Rico watched her metamorphosis from confusion to disbelief to realization. He'd taken a calculated risk and had no idea how she would react to his suggestion.

Lynda bit her lip. She knew what he was asking her without asking at all. He was leaving it entirely up to her. She literally and figuratively held the key in her hand.

She looked around the dance floor. Couples were locked in each others' arms. Older guests were gathering their belongings, taking the floral centerpieces and heading for the door. There were still a good many people laughing and partying. It seemed the wedding would go on for quite a while longer. All in all, one thing was clear. She and Rico could slip out and never be noticed.

What do you want from me, Lynda?

Lynda left him on the dance floor and headed back to her table. Rico hesitated briefly, then followed her. She picked up her purse, and slipped the card inside.

"Shall we go?" she asked.

Rico extended an arm toward the door. "By all means."

They rode up in the elevator in silence. Lynda's palms began to perspire. She was as nervous as could be, but her long years of training served her well: her face didn't show a thing.

Rico stayed well away from her in the elevator. He knew if he was close to her, he wouldn't wait for them to get to the room. It took all the control he had left not to pounce on her here and now. He couldn't remember ever needing a woman as badly as this. But that wasn't the problem, was it? It wasn't just any woman he needed, it was Lynda. Only Lynda.

And now was the time.

The elevator doors opened, and the two walked slowly down the hallway to the room. Lynda inserted the card into the door once, twice, three times, but the light never turned green, and the knob never turned. She wanted to scream with frustration, but she bit her lip and tried again.

"Let me," Rico said, and she handed him the key and stepped back from the door.

His first try was unsuccessful. Some people passed and smiled at their dilemma as Rico tried again. This time, the green light came on and the knob clicked open.

Rico stared at her for a long moment before opening the door. Lynda knew he was giving her a final out, a last chance to change her mind.

She didn't want to change her mind. She was as jittery as a cat on a hot tin roof, but she *most definitely* did not want to change her mind. She returned his steady gaze with a determined one of her own.

Rico opened the door. Lynda entered the room first. It was cool; the air conditioning had apparently been turned to the high setting. She flipped a switch. A dim light shone overhead. Rico entered behind her, and Lynda turned when she heard the door click shut.

They never made it to the bed. She fell into his arms. The impact pushed him up against the door. Rico kissed her long and hard. They were both beyond the preliminaries. He opened his mouth wider, and his tongue swept inside. Lynda whimpered with delight and matched his enthusiasm as she angled her head for better access.

He pulled at her short jacket, and it landed on the floor at their feet. In no time, her halter top was undone, and it fell forward to her waist. Lynda grabbed hold of his lapels and pulled his jacket off his shoulders until it trapped his arms. Rico stopped undressing her long enough to shrug out of the jacket and fling it somewhere into the room. All the time, their mouths were fused together in a hungry, devouring kiss.

He captured her breasts in his hands and caressed them, massaging each in turn. Lynda's breath was short, catching in her throat. Rico's lips moved from her mouth to first her neck, then on to the valley between her breasts. He cupped them together, and buried his face between them. His mouth laved first one, then the other, until she thought she would die from the pleasure.

But that was nothing compared to the tight contraction in her womb as he took her taut nipple into his mouth and suckled. His mouth was so hot, so wet. She held his face to her, and threaded her fingers through his hair. His skin was on fire; it seared her, branded her.

Like two crazed people, they tore at each other's clothing. Lynda almost ripped his shirt when the middle button wouldn't come apart. She pushed the shirt off of him and attacked his belt buckle as Rico finished pulling off her dress and slip.

She stood before him in only a white lace garter belt and panties. Rico rested his back against the door and savored the sight of her. He touched her face, then moved his hand to caress her cheek, her neck, her breasts and belly. He reached into the elastic waistband of her panties. Cupping her with the palm of his hand, he threaded his fingers through her soft blond curls. He smiled at the moist heat that greeted him and pressed his palm into her. Lynda's breath quickened, and like a moth to a flame, she moved into his touch.

Rico captured her mouth again in an all-consuming kiss at the same moment his fingers dipped into her. Lynda tensed with pleasure before her knees almost gave way. She was dizzy, breathless, lost to sensation as her body undulated in tandem to the movements of his hand. She knew if she had any presence of mind, she would be embarrassed, but his words of praise in her ear indicated he was as caught up in her delight as she.

His fingers continued their steady assault in an ever-increasing rhythm. Lynda clung to him for dear life.

She felt it rising within her, tiny bursts of heat rumbling beneath the surface much like the hot, molten lava of a sleeping volcano.

With his other hand, Rico reached up and gently rolled the tips of her breasts between his thumb and index finger. Sparkling points of light exploded in Lynda's brain, triggering a long, deep spasm of pleasure that shot through the very core of her body. She began to sway and shake uncontrollably as a shattering climax engulfed her.

Rico felt the tremors inside her and out. He continued to caress her until she cried out for him to stop. She collapsed against him. He turned with her in his arms, and pushed her firmly up against the door for support while he absorbed the aftershocks.

Lynda buried her face in his chest as she slowly drifted back to earth as she knew it. She had never in her life had as shattering an experience as this.

Slowly, shyly, she looked up into his eyes. Rico's face was taut with desire. Her own fulfillment had pushed him to the very edge, and it was blatantly clear that they weren't finished yet.

She didn't think it possible, but her body responded to that look, swelling once again with want. More than anything, she wanted to please him as much as he'd pleased her. She reached up to his waist and slowly released his zipper. She caressed him, wrapping her fingers around his width and length. He was so hot, so smooth, so... ready.

Rico felt her hesitation and read her mind.

"I won't hurt you," he said.

"I know," she answered, the movements of her hand becoming bolder. "I know."

Rico kissed her and moved a leg between her thighs. Lynda molded her body to his, rotating her hips into him, urging him to end their torment and join them together once and for all. She felt him reach between them and unsnap her garters. Her panties came off in one quick motion, and suddenly, finally, he was nestled between her legs.

Where he belonged.

Rico gritted his teeth. This is what he had been waiting for, aching for, since he'd first laid eyes on her. He pushed gently into her and gloried at her welcoming heat. Shutting his eyes in an attempt to gain control, to go slow with her, to make this moment last as long as possible, he adjusted his stance as inch by inch he joined their bodies together.

Lynda kissed his neck, and rubbed his back with her hands. She'd never felt so *full,* so totally owned and consumed by another person. She moved her hips, and was rewarded with a groan from Rico, as well as a warning not to move. She smiled her pleasure into his neck.

Around the edges of whatever mind Rico had left, an unwelcome thought intruded, one he should have, but hadn't considered before this very moment. Lynda moved, urging him on and he pushed farther into her until her warmth totally surrounded him with a liquid heat that was, at the same time, heaven and hell.

She began to whimper, and the thought fled with the sensations her sounds ignited. But as he began to move within her, the voice returned. He had to stop, ask the question now, right now, before it was too late....

"*Querida,*" he said softly. "Are you using anything?

"Do you mean birth control?"

"Yes."

"No."

She felt his body shudder.

"Don't you have . . . anything . . . ?" she asked in a prayerfully weak voice.

He shook his head into her neck.

Simultaneously they uttered the same expletive—he in Spanish, she in English.

Lynda collapsed against the door. Rico shut his eyes and separated himself from her. He moved away and rested his forehead on the cool metal door.

"Get dressed," he said.

"Rico—"

"Now. Please."

Lynda scooped up her clothing and almost ran into the bathroom. With shaking hands, she dressed herself so quickly, she didn't take the time to check her appearance in the mirror.

When she returned to the room, Rico was completely dressed. He caressed her cheek with his hand. "I'm sorry."

Lynda reached up and laid her own hand on top of his. She was distraught, unbalanced, aching for him, for herself.

"We could have—"

He put his fingers to her lips. "No, we couldn't. There are too many unwanted children in this world. I promised myself a long time ago I wouldn't add to them."

As he guided her out of the hotel room, down the elevator and into the lobby, the word reverberated in her mind.

Unwanted.

She didn't have the presence of mind to analyze what that meant to her, but she knew it was one word she would never use in relation to anything of his.

They didn't see Joe walk up behind them as they waited for the valet to bring the Mercedes around.

"There you two are!" Joe said. They both turned to look at the priest. "I was looking for you. Where'd you disappear to?"

"We went for a walk," Rico told his brother as the car pulled up.

He escorted Lynda around to the driver's side. Joe's gaze moved from Lynda to Rico and back again. Self-conscious and guilty as hell, she looked down at herself and realized her jacket was inside-out.

Lynda was mortified. She said a hasty good-night and slipped into the car. Rico bent over the window.

"I'm sorry for this," he whispered. "I didn't plan it very well. Hell, I didn't plan it at all."

"I know. I'm sorry, too."

He leaned in and brushed his lips against hers. "Good night, *querida*," he said.

"Good night." Lynda put the car into gear and tried her best not to speed away.

Rico stood back and watched the taillights disappear.

Joe rocked on his heels. "A walk, huh?"

Rico turned away, annoyed at his brother's interference. "Yeah. A walk."

Joe followed. "Seems to me you've got a real problem, Rico. A real, *big* problem."

"Is that a fact?"

"Yeah, it's a fact. If I were you—"

"You're not."

"No. But if I were..."

Joe trailed off and left his advice hanging. Rico stopped and turned to his brother. "Okay, let's have it. Tell me, Mr. Know-It-All, what would you do if you were me?"

"If I were you..." Joe picked at Rico's lapel and pulled off a long blond hair. He held it up in the air and released it. They both watched it float away. "I'd marry her, *hermano*." Joe reinforced his suggestion with a nod. "*Sí*, I'd marry her."

Eight

Marry her.

Like it was that simple.

Like it was even possible.

Rico mentally shook himself for the hundredth time since Joe first made that absurd suggestion. He had too much work to do, and to say the least, the thought distracted him. It was an insane idea, totally beyond the realm of reality, even if Lynda did condescend to seriously entertain it, which he knew she never would.

Then why did those two simple words repeat themselves over and over in his brain like a haunting litany?

He could just picture himself down on one knee asking her to give up her house in Palm Beach, to move onto the farm, to help him build his dream. What a joke! The picture lost focus when he tried to imagine Lynda taking care of an endless array of kids that were not her own, doing physically exhausting work with no servants to take over or help out.

And what would be her great reward for such a sacrifice?

Him.

All of him.

Everything he had to give. More.

Maybe even a couple of kids of their own.

And love. A lot of love.

For a lifetime . . .

Yeah, sure, Rico, keep dreaming.

She wanted him in bed, that much he did know. There was no way on earth she could have faked that response in the hotel room Saturday night. But more than that? He doubted it. An affair was all she was looking for. Her kind didn't marry his kind. He was good enough for a roll or two in the hay, but that was as far as it would go. He knew all about how that worked. He'd been this way before.

While he had to admit to himself that Lynda was in no way like Justine, he also had to admit that the situations were very similar. He hadn't changed that much in all these years; if anything, his life-style had become more simplistic. Lynda's life was worlds apart from the one to which he'd committed himself.

So why was he spending precious time dwelling on the possibility?

It was ridiculous, he told himself, impractical, unworkable. She'd call him crazy.

Put it out of your mind, man, or she'll be right.

An aide came to the door of his office, and he snapped to attention.

"Rico? Alan Levin is here," she said.

"Okay, tell him I'll be right there."

Alan was the inspector for Health and Human Services who Rico'd been avoiding for the past month or so. He had broken two appointments already this month, so he was not surprised that the man decided to drop in unexpectedly.

Rico was doing his damnedest to keep the shelter open until the fund-raiser was over. He couldn't afford to lose his license now. With all the bureaucratic nonsense involved in getting it back, the process could set all his plans back months, possibly years. But the house was a mess. The plumbing problem was the worst of it, but the roof also leaked during and after each rain. The water damage showed on the walls, and there was little he could do to hide it.

Steve wasn't lying when he'd said they could close him down for such violations, but he needed every dime for the down payment on the farm. He wished he'd had some money in reserve to patch up the trouble spots and keep this place afloat—literally and figuratively—until he could get the financing for the farm, but he didn't have the extra money, and large, windfall donations just didn't happen every day.

And then there were the extra kids . . .

"Hi, Alan. How's it going?" Rico said as he walked into the hallway to greet the man.

"Not bad, not bad. Hope you don't mind my dropping in like this. I know how busy you are."

Rico let the barb slip by; the man was entitled. "No, not at all. Where do you want to begin?"

"Upstairs?"

Rico extended his arm toward the stairway, "You know the way."

Alan climbed the stairs. Having never been particularly religious—even with a priest for a brother—

Rico was surprised to find himself saying a short prayer as he followed behind.

It couldn't hurt, he thought…and he needed all the help he could get.

It was time to take the bull by the horns.

So to speak.

Lynda slammed her car door and crunched her way across the pebblestone driveway to the front door of the shelter. She was determined. The time had come for her to take charge. She was that sort of person, wasn't she? Since when did she sit around and wait for someone else to make things happen? No, she was the catalyst, and if she and Rico were ever going to be alone—really alone—it was up to her to arrange it.

Taking a deep breath, she let herself in. It had been three days since Elena's wedding. She'd spent the entire day Sunday hiding in her house. Rico had called but she'd been too embarrassed to even answer the phone. She'd let her answering machine pick up his message.

She had never thought of herself as a sexual person, but the past three nights had produced the most erotic dreams she had ever had—or ever imagined existed.

This had to stop. Once and for all, she would get this out of her system. The thought of making love with him was obsessing her to the point where she hardly thought of anything else. It couldn't go on. She wouldn't let it.

And if all went well, tomorrow night the torture would end.

She planned to invite him to her house for dinner, ostensibly to firm up all the finishing touches for the fund-raiser. But that was only her excuse to get him up to her house. Once he was there, she planned to seduce him with wine, moonlight and the skimpiest negligee she could get her hands on. No way would they be interrupted tomorrow night. Nothing would stop them. Nothing. She'd even bought a box of condoms.

Lynda stopped short outside of Rico's office. There was someone inside with him, and the door was slightly ajar. Not wanting to eavesdrop, she made her way toward the kitchen in hopes of finding Mrs. Ortiz. She wanted to express her delight in the wedding, feeling a bit guilty about running off without saying goodbye.

"Give me two weeks."

She came to a halt at the sound of Rico's voice. Against her better judgment, she leaned an ear forward.

"I'll get the plumbing fixed, and at least have some patch work done on the roof," Rico said.

"I've already given you two warnings on this, Rico. What's two weeks going to do for you?"

'I'll come up with the money. I promise.''

"You've promised before."

"And I've come through. No?"

"Yes ... but always late. I have a job to do, too, Rico, and you know I'll work with you, but I've got pressure from my boss. He thinks I'm too lenient with you guys."

"Two weeks, Alan. Lose the paperwork, whatever it takes. It'll be done.

Alan sighed. "Okay, okay. Two weeks. Now, what about these extra kids? You know I've looked the other way before, but you're only supposed to house ten, and you hardly have the room for them. Fourteen is totally out of the question."

"They'll also be gone by the time the plumbing work is finished."

"Another promise?" Alan asked.

"Yeah. Another one." Lynda heard the smile in Rico's voice.

A chair scraped backward. The man was leaving. Lynda tiptoed toward the front door and turned the knob just as Rico and Alan walked out of the office.

"Hi," she said, pretending to be only just arriving.

"Hello," Rico replied.

He introduced Alan to Lynda. Alan extended his hand and they shook.

"It's a pleasure," Alan said. "I've heard about the fund-raiser. Is it going well?"

"Very well," she said. "We're going to make a lot of money for Home Sweet Home."

"Good, good. I'm happy to hear it." Alan turned to Rico and slapped him on the back. "Two weeks."

Rico nodded his affirmation. "Two weeks."

Alan said his goodbyes and left Rico and Lynda standing in the hallway. Rico stared into the empty space for a moment, then turned and walked back into his office. Lynda followed.

"What was that all about?" she asked.

"Inspection. We were overdue."

"What did he say?" she asked, feigning ignorance.

"We've got two weeks to fix the place up, or he's going to parcel out the kids to other agencies."

"No!"

"Yes."

"Why?"

"Because it's been like this too long. His boss is on him, and I can't even blame the guy. He's worked with me in the past, looking the other way when necessary." Rico ran a hand through his hair. "I've got to patch this place up. We're too close to give it all up now."

"What about the money that's coming in from the fund-raiser? Can't you tap into that?"

"No way. The bank's holding on to it for the down payment on the farm. I'm not going to do anything to jeopardize that," he said.

"What are you going to do?"

"Don't worry about it. I'll find a way."

Lynda walked over to him and placed a hand on his arm. "Can I help?"

Rico smiled. He covered her hand with his own. "Thank you, but no. I'll work it out. Two weeks is a long time in this business. A lot of things can happen."

"Like?"

"Oh, I don't know. Like a fat unsolicited donation from a recently deceased dowager who once took a tour of Home Sweet Home, fell in love with my face and remembered me in her will." She laughed at his creative imagery. "You know, something like that."

"You're insane," she said, but filed the thought away in her mind.

"Yeah," he said, and caressed her cheek with his fingertips. "Absolutely *loco*."

Lynda leaned forward as his head descended. Their lips brushed against one another gently back and forth. Rico slanted his head to the side and captured her mouth in a long, slow, thirst-quenching kiss.

"I've missed you," he said.

"Me, too."

Her face was slightly flushed. He wanted to kiss her again, and again, and again...but now more than ever was not the time. His mind was filled with what he should be doing, and those thoughts warred with what he wanted to be doing.

A cloud descended over his face, and Lynda moved back from him. She didn't want to start something that they once more couldn't finish. No, this time she would put her plan into action.

"What are you doing tomorrow night?" she asked.

Rico flipped a page on his desk calendar. "Nothing special. What do you have in mind?"

"I'd like to go over the final arrangements for the dinner-dance."

"Sure. Where and when?"

"My house? Seven o'clock?"

Rico's heart flip-flopped in his chest. He'd never been invited to her house. The thought enticed him and scared the hell out of him at the same time. He stared at her for a moment, but her face was blank, innocent, and gave no indication of her intent.

"Sure."

"I'll give you directions."

She picked up a pad from his desk and scribbled something down, then handed it to Rico. He looked at the paper.

"Are you familiar with the area?" she asked.

"I'll find it."

"Great," she said. Cool to the end, Lynda smiled, even though her stomach felt as if it were filled with Mexican jumping beans. "Then I'll see you tomorrow. Don't eat. We'll have dinner together."

"Can you cook?" he asked. As if it mattered.

"Steaks, salad, that sort of thing. Okay with you?"

"Sounds perfect."

"See you then."

"See you then."

She scurried out the door like a squirrel with a satchel of acorns. He wondered what she was thinking or planning.

It didn't really matter, did it? he thought. He smiled broadly.

This was *it*.

Rico was as nervous as a teenager on prom night. He'd almost stopped at a florist to pick up flowers, but felt it was too corny and drove away. Instead, he'd picked up a bottle of the California white wine he knew she liked.

He found the house with no trouble; her directions were precise. He pulled onto the concrete driveway, cut the engine and admired her home. The house was white, modernistic with a pointed, California-style wraparound deck. It wasn't very big, but the skylights, glass walls and doors gave it an open, airy look. Sitting back, he took in the perfect setting, wondering, not for the first time, what the hell he was getting himself into.

Lynda glanced out the beveled glass side panel of the front door. Nervously she rubbed her hands together as she waited for him to get out of the car. What was he doing just sitting there?

Her stomach churned, and not just with anticipation for the evening ahead. She had done something today that she hoped would please him, but with Rico, one never knew. Erotic dreams hadn't kept her up last night, but worry about his plight had. Two weeks was a sickeningly short amount of time to come up with the thousands of dollars needed to repair the shelter.

He'd said he would handle it, but how? Most of the heavy donors who could be counted on in a pinch had already made huge pledges for the fund-raiser. There just wasn't any stone left to turn.

It was her business to know these things, but not her business to tell Rico. Still, she couldn't stop herself from getting involved. She had a deep desire to see him succeed with his dream, and she would do anything she possibly could to help him.

So, she did. With a call to her banker this morning, Lynda had become that secret donor he'd conjured up. Dee thought it was a great idea, all so mysterious and romantic, but Lynda was not so sure that Rico would feel the same way. Nevertheless, she had to tell him, and the thought of how he would react was making her nauseous.

Wine bottle in hand, Rico made his way to the front door and rang the bell. Immediately the door swung open, as if she were standing behind it waiting for his arrival.

"I'm late," he said, apologizing before she could accuse him.

"It's okay. I saw you sitting in the car. I thought something was wrong."

"Nothing's wrong. I was just admiring the view."

Lynda accepted the proffered bottle of wine and thanked him as she led the way into the living room. She excused herself, and he watched her seemingly float from the room. She wore a mauve and purple silk caftan printed with an Oriental design. It caressed her body as she moved, and jealously, he wanted to do the same.

Left to his own devices, Rico observed his surroundings. The room was decorated in pale tones of peach, white and cornflower blue, dominated by a wraparound sofa in the center. There were accent tables and a chair in the corner. And lots of plants. For the most part, it was underfurnished, which only added to the feeling of space and freedom.

The entire back wall was glass, opening upon a deck that overlooked the ocean. He walked out onto the deck and paced slowly back and forth. The sky was darkening into twilight. He leaned into the deck railing and lifted his face to the cool ocean breeze.

This was the life, he thought. Her home looked as if it belonged in a layout for an architectural magazine. He was impressed, and perhaps a bit depressed, though not surprised. It was the kind of place in which he'd always pictured her. No doubt about it, she belonged here; she fit. The style of the place, the subtle color scheme, the feeling of *softness* it exuded, all contributed to his image of who and what Lynda was.

His mouth formed a self-mocking half smile. He had to stop himself from laughing out loud at the absurdity of the direction of his recent thoughts. It didn't take a genius to figure out that one thing was certain—any and all thought of her walking away from this was self-delusion of the worst kind.

Lynda stepped onto the deck carrying a tray with wine and cheese.

"Your home is beautiful," he said.

"Thank you," she said, and set the tray down on the table. "It's small by Palm Beach standards, but it's the first place I've ever lived in that's totally mine."

"It suits you."

"Like the car?"

Rico grinned. "Yeah, like the car."

"Were the directions all right?" she asked, changing the subject.

"Fine. We had some trouble down at the shelter. That's why I was late."

"What trouble?" she asked as she handed him the wine glass.

"Two nights ago, a woman who lived a few blocks away knocked on the door around three in the morning. She had four kids with her. Her grandchildren, she said." He tasted the wine and continued, "She had to have some minor surgery in the morning. Her daughter was supposed to return for them, but never showed up. She couldn't leave them alone, so..."

"So, she brought them to Home Sweet Home."

"Yeah. We have this reputation."

"I know." She smiled at him, a smile filled with the pride she felt for him and the importance of his work.

"Anyway," Rico said. He moved to the cushioned lounge chair and sat down on the edge. "Even though we had a full house, we took the kids in rather than let them get parceled out to foster homes. The grandmother will be out of the hospital in about a week, and she promised to take them back."

"So what happened?"

"The mother showed up this evening just before I was about to leave to come here. She wanted the kids, and I wouldn't release them to her. Things got nasty. She called the police."

"What did you do?"

"I know all the cops in the area. It was settled soon."

"What will happen to her?"

"She'll settle up when her mother gets out of the hospital and picks them up. I didn't know her from Adam, and I wasn't going to just turn them over to her. Besides, the kids didn't want to go. Kids know what's right for them, sometimes better than we do, you know."

Lynda thought about her own childhood, and nodded. "Do things like this happen often?"

"All the time." They stared at each other for a long moment. "Alan Levin gave me a hard time about the extra kids, but I got a two-week reprieve out of him."

"Just like the plumbing?"

He nodded. "Yep. Just like the plumbing."

"Any mysterious donor show up yet?" she asked.

"No. Not yet."

"Rico..."

He took a sip of wine. "Hmm?"

"I'd like to be the one."

"What one?"

"The donor. I'd like to give you the money to fix the house."

A chill, cold and clammy, ran down his back. Rico slowly placed his wineglass on the table. He didn't expect it, not from her, but perhaps he should have. Visions of Justine's laughing face flashed through his mind. His stomach pitched, and the taste of the wine turned sour in his mouth.

He stood and turned his back to her as he looked out over the dark ocean glistening with the early rays of moonlight. He shut his eyes to gain control, but all it did was disorient him, and he had to grab hold of the deck railing for balance. He felt sick.

"Is that what tonight is all about?" he asked softly.

Lynda stood and moved next to him. "I don't know what you mean."

He turned to her, his face a mask of hurt and anger. "No? Then tell me this. Why did you invite me here tonight?"

Lynda moved her eyes away from his penetrating gaze. Her heart was pounding. Obviously she wasn't handling this well. She knew he might be reluctant to take her money, but there was something else here, something deeper, more involved. The look on his face was stone-cold, almost scary.

"Why do you think?"

He took hold of her arms and forced her to look at him. "I *thought* it was because you wanted us to be alone . . . to be together. I didn't think you planned to pay me for the privilege as well."

"How could you think that! I only want to help you."

"Help me? With money? I told you more than once I don't need you for money. I can get it myself. It might take a little longer, but I can do it. That's not what I need, Lynda, especially from you."

"What *do* you need from me?" She couldn't hide the hurt in her voice. Why couldn't he understand? Why couldn't he see her offer for what it was?

He released her and moved away. "If you have to ask that . . ."

Rico stepped back into the house and made his way toward the door. Lynda panicked as she saw him reach for the doorknob. This couldn't be happening! She had planned this evening right down to the last possible minute. It wasn't working out at all. Everything was falling apart around her. She couldn't let it. She wouldn't. She ran into the house after him.

"Rico!"

He turned, the look on his face implacable. She didn't fully understand why he was so angry. Money was an asset, to be sure, but also a tool, to be used when needed. She certainly wasn't *buying* him. Couldn't he see that? Perhaps it had to do with his Hispanic male pride. Whatever the case, she was dead sure it was the very last thing she'd intended to do, and if there was any way out of this, she had better find it quickly.

"Please don't go."

"Lynda, this is not a game," he said. "I'm not an object on the Monopoly board that can be moved, bought and sold on a whim. If I stay here with you, it's because you want me. *Me,* for myself."

Lynda walked up to him, and slowly wound her arms around his neck. She pushed to her tiptoes and brushed her lips against his cheek.

"You must know. I want you...for you...." Emotion welled in her throat, and her already scratchy voice became even more raspy. "Forget about the money. I just want you to...stay." Her lips parted and found his.

Rico didn't move; couldn't move. Her warm breath fanned his mouth, his cheek, his neck, as she continued to nuzzle a response out of him. His mind told him he should leave, he really should: He didn't need this.

But his body was another story.

She kissed him, pushing past his unresponsive lips with her tongue, until, of its own volition, his mouth opened and gave way to the heat and feel of her yielding softness. Giving up the futile fight, he reached up and cupped the back of her head with one hand, while the other skimmed down to her bottom and pressed her body into his.

All pretenses and thoughts of reality aside, this was the reason he was here tonight. This was what he'd dreamed of, longed for. And if this was all there ever would be...then, fine, okay, so be it. He tilted her head and kissed her, a full, openmouthed kiss that totally consumed her, taking all she offered and more.

Lynda's tongue mated with his in a slow, timeless ritual that set her mind blank to all but sensation. Her heart began to beat faster. She could hear her blood pulsing through her veins as it pounded in her ears. She pushed herself higher, into him, winding one leg around his thigh in an attempt to wrap herself around him.

Passion exploded between them like a match to high octane gasoline. Rico picked her up, scooped her into his arms as if she were a weightless child and carried her out onto the deck. Without a word, he laid her down on the chaise lounge, and lifted the caftan over her head. Underneath, she wore only a pale ivory satin teddy that caught the reflection of the moonlight and cast an ethereal glow around her body.

Rico pulled at the thin straps and exposed her breasts to the night air. He ran the palms of his hands across her nipples, and they puckered expectantly. Not one to disappoint, he leaned down and feathered each with the tip of his tongue. He then took her into the heat of his mouth and suckled her with such gentle force that uncontrollable spasms of pure pleasure rippled inside her with each glorious tug.

Lynda ran her fingers through his thick hair, encouraging him by arching her back. As his hands reached to discard the teddy entirely, his lips roamed down her torso to the soft skin of her belly, and below. His hands grabbed hold of her hips, and he reached beneath her to separate her legs.

Rico leaned back slightly to view her naked beauty. She lay across the lounge in wanton splendor, ready for him, open to him, unashamed, waiting, wanting...

"Rico..."

He shook his head. "No more talk."

Their eyes met and held. Lynda's breath was short, her lips parted as she watched his eyes darken to an ebony more black than the night sky above.

He threaded his fingers through her blond curls and massaged that special spot with the pad of his thumb. He was rewarded with a whimper, and smiled at her uninhibited response. Then his mouth replaced his fingers as he kissed her, nipped her, licked her, until she cried out with pleasure.

A ball of fire spun around and around inside Lynda, growing large, dropping lower until its heat and all her concentration was centered on the spot where his mouth met her body. There was no thought, only feeling—deep, savage, undeniable feeling that roared in her ears and burst from her soul like an exploding nova. She gasped for air, and opened her eyes to the starry sky as the contractions took her on a roller-coaster ride of sublime pleasure.

She called his name out loud, once, twice, three times, dragging the last vowel out into a cry in the night.

And then, silence.

The trip back to reality was slow, luxurious and thoroughly satisfying. Lynda reached down to Rico, and he moved his body onto hers. Their eyes roamed each other's face, as his lips slowly descended to capture her mouth in a sealing kiss.

Rico stood and began to strip his clothing. Lynda watched from her languid position on the lounge. His body gleamed in the moonlight, perfect—and ready— in every way.

It was then she saw the tattoo. Centered below his waist was a small heart pierced top-through-bottom with an arrow that pointed downward to the precise location of his erection. Lynda traced it with the tip of her fingernail.

"I like it," she said. A slow smile graced her lips as her finger completed its descent. "But I don't really think directions are necessary."

"Very funny," he said, then lay down next to her on the lounge, face-to-face.

"Don't move," Lynda whispered as she scrambled off the lounge.

"What? Lynda—"

"Stay right there. I'll be right back."

Rico muttered an especially meaningful expletive as she literally ran into the house. His body was in overdrive—hot, hard and revved to the point of explosion. What the hell was she up to now?

Good to her word, she was back in a flash. She walked over to him, almost shyly, and he sat up.

"What is that you have in your hand?" he asked.

Lynda held out a cellophane-wrapped box. Rico took it from her and looked down at the giant economy-size box of condoms. A thoroughly male grin split his face.

"Thirty-six?" he asked, unable to control the smile in his voice.

"I didn't want us to run out."

"I can see that." He laughed and shook his head. Pulling her to him, he kissed the tip of her nose. "I'll do my best, *querida*. But maybe not all tonight?"

She hugged him, grateful that his light mood had returned, grateful that he looked at her with want and desire, not the disappointment that had been evident on his face before. She ran her hands down his back, his sides, his well-formed buttocks, down to his tight, muscled thighs.

The laughter died in Rico's throat as she wrapped her hand around his length. Like a curious child, she touched him tentatively, with cotton-soft strokes of her fingertips. Rico swallowed hard. He stared at the stars overhead, forcing his body to focus on the night, to stay in control just a little longer. With the promise of fulfillment in sight, he let her have her way.

Lynda caressed him with both hands, watching herself as she touched him, driving herself crazy with the imagery of their bodies joined together.

"*Querida.*"

She looked up into his eyes and saw the intensity of his need. He didn't have to ask.

"Yes. Oh, yes, Rico..."

He opened one of the packets, and Lynda stayed his hand. The pleasure of her touch was so intense, it was just short of agony. He held his breath as she performed the intimate gesture for him. With control beyond his wildest imagination, he entered her slowly. Lynda arched her back to receive him, opening herself to him, until he was completely joined to her. She buried her face in his neck as the sensation of fullness engulfed her.

Rico kissed her, his tongue imitating the increasingly more energetic movements of his body. Lynda matched his enthusiasm stroke for stroke, until they were lost in a rhythm all their own, lost in that dreamlike, utopian state of being reserved only for powerful gods and passionate lovers.

With all his might, Rico tried to prolong their pleasure, to bring her back to the heights and beyond, but his body refused to listen. It had waited too long, been denied too long to endure any further sacrifice. With a groan that started deep in his throat, he gave up the battle and allowed the wave to take him home.

Lynda held him close to her. She couldn't speak. Her throat was swollen with emotion. Making love with him was all she had dreamed it would be, and more. Fantasies were wonderful, and erotic dreams could bring her to a fevered pitch of anticipation. But nothing—nothing—could have prepared her for the power and beauty of this moment.

She looked into his eyes and saw the same wonder reflected there. They didn't speak; there was nothing left to say. Their bodies had communicated in the most primal, elemental way God had created.

It was over, yet in so many ways, it was just beginning.

Without a word, Lynda left him and walked, unabashedly naked, to the table. She felt powerful and in control, like a butterfly released from its cocoon into a bright spring day. With languid movements, she poured them each a glass of wine. Slowly she returned to him and sat on the edge of the lounge chair. She handed him his glass, then held hers out to him for a toast.

Rico clinked their glasses as he eyed this new, self-absorbed, satiated Lynda with a puzzled eye.

"To us," she said, and sipped at the wine.

"To us," he answered, and did the same.

Lynda leaned forward and kissed the wine from his lips. Her breasts grazed his chest, and her eyes fluttered shut at contact. Rico wrapped his fingers around the stem of her glass and took it from her, carefully placing both on the wooden deck. He reached for her, and she willingly went into his arms. In no time at all, they were locked once again in a heated embrace, their hands and mouths moving haphazardly over each other.

Lynda pushed him down on the lounge and straddled him, enormously pleased with his look of surprise. Encouraged by his reaction to her boldness, she leaned over him, an arm on either side of his head. She threw her head back and closed her eyes for a moment, lifting her face to the stars as she savored the feel of his body touching hers in all the right places.

Rico watched as she tested her feminine power on him. He was bemused, he was enchanted...maybe he was even a little in love. She stared at him from beneath heavy lids that couldn't mask the brilliant blue eyes ablaze with passion.

"Mmm..." The purring sound emerged from deep in her throat as she rotated her hips against him. "You know...we still have...thirty-five...to go," she whispered into his ear.

Rico nipped at her lobe and wet it with the tip of his tongue. "Thirty-six."

"What—"

Rico reached over her. He rummaged through the pockets of his discarded trousers and held up a square foil packet for her inspection.

Lynda grinned. "I see you were prepared."

"Ever the Boy Scout," he answered.

Lynda plucked the packet out of his hand. "Well," she said, "I was a Girl Scout, and we had a saying of our own, you know."

"Really? What was that?"

She tore open the packet. "Waste not, want not."

Nine

I'll tell him tonight.

Lynda stood on the deck. It was midday, and the sun blazed overhead, tempered only by the ocean's steady breeze. Her gauzy white beach robe whipped around her legs. Through mirrored sunglasses, she watched Rico as he dived directly into the waves.

Tonight was the dinner-dance, the final phase in the fund-raising event for Home Sweet Home. She had invited Rico to spend the day with her on the beach, and they planned to leave from here for the benefit at the country club.

He turned and waved from the shoreline before running back into the rough surf. Lynda waved back with both arms. It had been two weeks since they'd made love for the first time, and her body still tingled whenever she looked at him. Each day was worse than the day before. She *longed* for him. It sounded like such an old-fashioned word, but it perfectly described the feeling that had taken up residence in the region of her heart.

She responded to him like a child: happy when he was happy, disturbed or worried when he was worried. Her moods reflected his to the point where she could barely think of anything else *but* him.

Thank God it wasn't affecting her business. Since her business was *his* business right now, it seemed only to make her sharper in her work, more intent on making the event succeed.

She'd fallen in love with him, and while she should be happy as a clam about it, she felt instead as if a heavy stone was wedged in her rib cage. And why? Because the greatest barrier between them was something that wouldn't go away: Her secret donation to Home Sweet Home.

She'd tried to stop the bank from making the anonymous donation to the shelter. The very next morning, after Rico had left, she'd run to the phone and had called her bank to cancel the transaction, but her ever-efficient representative had already sent it on its way. Overnight express.

Barely an hour after Rico had arrived back at Home Sweet Home, he'd called her. Guess what? he'd said. Fate was on their side. A large, unsolicited donation had been sitting on his desk when he'd walked in. He'd said he had to call her to tell her—and maybe gloat a bit as well? Magnanimous with the check in his hand, he'd thanked her for her generous offer. He'd overreacted, he'd said, and had apologized. Now that he had the money to fix up the place, the point was moot anyway, wasn't it?

Sure it was.

She should have told him right then and there, she knew that now. But he had been so contrite, so adorably affectionate, and she had still been suffering from the residual effects of their intense night of lovemaking. What harm would it do to wait a day or two, then tell him?

Lynda turned away from the ocean and lay down on the chaise lounge. She took off her glasses and lifted her face to the sun. Its heat penetrated her skin, but couldn't melt the icicle of dread around her heart. A day or two had become a week, then two weeks, and still she hadn't been able to tell him the truth. It stuck in her throat and had been lodged there ever since.

Every day she told herself today was the day to tell him, but every day he'd look at her with those Spanish eyes of his, and it had been all too easy to melt into his arms, pretend she was Scarlett O'Hara, and promise herself that "tomorrow is another day."

She really, truly, couldn't put it off any longer. The thought that he might never find out notwithstanding, if they were ever going to have any type of relationship beyond this fund-raiser, it had to begin with a clean slate. She was not a deceitful person, and the lie was hanging hot and heavy between them, almost as hot and heavy as the constant desire to be naked, in bed, making love.

Almost, but not quite.

She'd tell him tonight, after the dinner, after it was all over, after it was a success. She had what she felt was the perfect plan. She would add the donation to her bill for the fund-raiser. She'd tell Rico it wasn't a gift, only a loan, and now that he had the money, he could pay her back. He might get initially annoyed, but she was sure he would relent in the end.

She hoped.

"Wake up, sleepyhead," Rico said, dripping water onto her. He sat beside her on the edge of the lounge, leaned over and gave her a wet kiss. "If I didn't know better, I'd say you didn't sleep much last night."

"I didn't." She reached up to him and stroked his wet hair back from his face. "Something kept waking me."

"Hmm..." he said as he nuzzled her neck. Pulling the drawstring, he lowered her collar to reveal her bikini top. "I wonder what."

His wetness cooled her heated skin, and she arched her body to give him better access. "I'll give you a hint," she said as she caressed his chest.

She moved her hand lower to the waistband of his bathing suit. Slipping her fingers inside, she brushed them against him, and his body reacted immediately to her touch.

"Oh, *that*..." he said, and moved on top of her. Rico kissed her neck, wetting her with his body as well as his tongue. "I want you," he whispered in her ear.

She closed her eyes. The sound of his voice and the portent of his words made her weak, and she wished the world and everything in it would disappear around them, leaving them alone to explore each other inch by delicious inch.

The sound of people's laughter rose from the beach. They looked up to see a group walking by.

"Let's go inside," Rico said.

He drew her up from the chair and led her into the bedroom. The bed was still in disarray. Lynda had cancelled her housekeeper's services for the day, as was becoming her habit whenever Rico was around. She knew he'd be uncomfortable with someone else in the house, and selfishly, she didn't want to share his space with anyone.

Rico stood in the middle of the room facing Lynda. He pulled off his wet suit and stepped out of it. Lynda slipped the robe off and let it fall to her feet. She walked up to him, stopping just short of touching her body to his.

Rico reached around her and unhooked her skimpy top. It fell to the floor between them. Gently he grazed the back of his knuckles across her breasts. Tiny tingles chilled her sun-warmed skin, and her nipples puckered in response. With one hand cupping each side of her full breasts, he drew her to him. His mouth descended onto hers, and his thumbs flicked back and forth in time to the thrust of his tongue in her mouth.

Lynda moaned and wrapped her arms around his waist, pushing herself into the heat of his hard, aroused body. Droplets of water were still beaded on his back, and she massaged each with the palms of her hand. She nipped the skin on his chest and breathed deeply. He smelled of the sea and his own, unique scent of man.

Rico walked backward with Lynda in his arms until the backs of his knees hit the edge of the bed. He swung her around, and she lost her balance, falling onto the mattress. He stood above her, one knee on the bed, poised and ready, so very ready, to make her part of him.

He bent down and untied one side of her bikini bottom. With a flick of his wrist, he exposed her soft blond mound to his view. As if in slow motion, he moved his hand between her thighs and caressed the smooth skin, skimming upward, entwining his fingers in her damp curls. Eagerly she opened her legs and gave herself to his touch.

Rico's head was spinning with desire, in a dream-like state of unreality. Part of him could not believe his good fortune to be here with Lynda, her body so ripe and waiting for him. The other part of him demanded no thought at all, only instinct, only action, to appease this splendid hunger that had gripped him by its jaws and hung on for dear life.

He shook his head, more to himself than to her. Lynda raised herself on her arms and looked at him. She reached up to touch that part of him that spoke so eloquently of his desire for her. She stroked him with her hand, then moved closer and kissed him.

Rico shut his eyes tightly, trying to control his body's reaction to the pleasure-pain her mouth inflicted. He ran his fingers through her long blond hair, caressing her scalp as she continued her assault on his senses. And when it became too much to bear, he pulled her away and came down onto the bed, covering her with his body.

His mouth found hers open, wet and ready for him, and his tongue plunged inside at the exact moment that he thrust himself into her welcoming warmth.

They made love as if the house were on fire, but the only fire burning was the one inside each of them, an insatiable flame that threatened to consume them both. Lynda brought her knees up and wrapped her legs high around his waist, egging him on, urging him with each movement to push deeper, stay longer, withdraw slower, until her body caught his rhythm and ran with it into a shattering, blissful climax. She shouted out her praise and delight, the sound of which helped take him over the edge with her.

Rico turned to his side with her in his arms. It took a long moment for both of them to catch their breath, and when they did, their eyes met, held and said things to each other that they were not yet able to articulate.

For a very long time, they were silent. Lynda stroked his cheek with her fingertips, then his jaw and around to his earlobe, finally toying with the small gold stud anchored there. It was amazing how she still ached for him, even now, when her body was spent and satisfied. She tilted her mouth up to him, and he kissed her, a sweet, poignant kiss, filled with enormous emotion.

She rolled her body onto his.

"We'll be late," he said.

"I don't care," she answered.

He kissed her again, holding her head with his hands. Lynda broke free. She slid down to his chest and lower, pausing by the infamous tattoo, kissing, nipping, wetting him with her tongue as she traveled south.

"Lynda..."

She heard the warning in his voice, but continued her assault, determined to make love with him one more time.

Lynda heard another voice, too, this one, her conscience warning her that time was running out. She shut her ears to the summons. This was what she wanted, this was what she needed. All the rest didn't matter. Her time was here, now, with him, and she didn't want to waste a minute of it thinking about anything that might mar the beauty of the moment.

She closed her eyes as she took him into her mouth.

I'll tell him tonight.

* * *

Lynda wore white, a body-shaped designer dress that stopped just above her knees. It had a scalloped edging along its décolletage with off-the-shoulder, stand-away sleeves. Her hair was loose, a shimmering cascade of long blond waves framing her face. People turned to stare as she moved around the room, and with good reason. She was classy, elegant, sophisticated, beautiful... and his.

That was the way he thought of her. His. *His woman.* Rico smiled inwardly. He'd thought the days of that old macho Hispanic image of himself were long gone. It surprised him to find that it had only been dormant, hiding, waiting for the right woman to trigger all those possessive emotions again. But here it was, that protective feeling, the one that said she belonged to him, body and soul.

He watched her work the room, smiling, shaking hands, cajoling the country-club types to fill out one more pledge card, take one more raffle ticket. She was animated, charming, the epitome of the perfect hostess. Only he knew the high color on her cheeks reflected their afternoon of passion as much, if not more, than her enthusiasm for the evening ahead.

He looked down and saw Tomás toddling along not more than two feet behind Lynda. The boy was outfitted in a miniature blue blazer, gray trousers and white shirt with a pint-size red bow tie. It had been Lynda's idea to include the residents of Home Sweet Home in the festivities. More and more, Rico was coming to realize her generosity of spirit, as well as her commitment to him and his people.

Together, they worked out a plan to transport everyone to the country club. It was decided that the children would attend the cocktail party only, so that the little ones could be back home and in bed at a reasonable time. Mrs. Ortiz and the rest of the staff handled the supervision of the children. Each child was decked out in his Sunday best and bubbly with excitement. The event had been the major topic of conversation at the shelter for the last two weeks.

Tomás tugged at Lynda's hem. Without interrupting her conversation with a very dignified older gentleman, Lynda reached down and lifted the boy into her arms. He hugged her and rested his weary head on her shoulder. A waiter carrying a tray of crystal flute glasses filled with champagne weaved through the crowd. Rico watched as Tomás lifted his head. His eyes lit up as the waiter approached. Recognizing an accident waiting to happen, Rico moved through the crowd and pulled Tomás from Lynda's arms seconds before disaster struck. Catching Mrs. Ortiz's eye, he handed the boy off to her.

Lynda turned toward him to thank him; their eyes met and held. His gaze caressed her, and her face flushed. She smiled tentatively, hesitating only a moment before resuming her hostessing responsibilities.

Rico grinned at her discomfort. She'd more than surprised him this afternoon in bed. He had no doubt she'd surprised herself as well. Of course, he'd known from the first that beneath that cool facade was hidden a passionate nature. But the tigress he'd encountered today was something to behold. It was as if a genie had been let out of a long discarded bottle. She revealed a side of herself that he was sure she had not even known existed.

No doubt about it—she had called the shots, had orchestrated each touch, each caress, each position as if she had sat up the night before and planned the strategy. Lynda had made love to him with such un-inhibited imagination that he could do no more than lie back and enjoy it.

Enjoy it, he had. He couldn't help but wonder what triggered such aggressiveness on her part. Whatever it was, he wished they'd bottle it. Just looking at her prance around the room was making him ache with the memory. His body was still throbbing from the after-effects of her ingenuity. And anxious for more.

"Isn't this delightful?"

Rico turned to see Barbara Johnson and Megan Palmer standing behind him. He smiled and greeted both ladies.

"Lynda has done such a wonderful job," Barbara continued. "Don't you agree?"

"Without a doubt. She's a very talented lady," he said with a smile. They had no idea *how* talented.

"Do you have your speech ready?" she asked. "They'll expect you to say a few words when they award you with the plaque."

"Yes, ma'am," Rico said, and patted the breast pocket of his tuxedo jacket. "I know exactly what I'm going to say."

"Wonderful! I'm so pleased with how things are going. Aren't you pleased, Megan?" Barbara asked.

"Yes." The ever-efficient Megan looked straight at Rico. "I think you have a wonderful organization here, Mr. Alvarez. I had the pleasure of taking a tour of the shelter recently, and I was very, very im-pressed."

"Well, thank you, Mrs. Palmer. I'm happy to hear that." He had heard about the tour, though he wasn't present at the time. It was the day before the anonymous check arrived. He was more than convinced that Megan was the one.

Megan smiled. She graced him with a knowing look as well as a conspiratorial squeeze of his arm before she moved away. That clinched it. Without a doubt, she was his mysterious donor. He wasn't surprised by the fact that she'd acted anonymously. Many ladies liked to give money that way, sometimes so that their husbands wouldn't be involved. He didn't know about Meg Palmer's marital situation, but he was more than grateful to her for bailing him out.

The plumbing work was proceeding quickly and effectively. It was amazing how fast things could be accomplished once the money was there. Alan Levin had been in last week with a big smile on his face. It was satisfying to Rico to be able to keep his word.

The extra children were also gone. Their grandmother had returned for them and had told him that their mother was coming back to live with her. He'd wished them all well, and left the door open for any future help he could give them. He knew from experience that these situations didn't always have happy endings.

Things were going well; sometimes he thought too well. He'd been astonished by the amount of money Lynda had been able to raise with this event. He had more than he needed for the down payment for the farm, and the bank was working with him to finance the renovation work. It seemed that in the short time he had known Lynda, she had brought him luck...and something more he was afraid to say aloud lest he jinx it.

Since the first night they'd made love on her deck, he'd been fantasizing about a possible life together.

Sure there were problems, but what they felt for each other was deep, and true. Problems could be worked out if two people wanted it enough.

He trusted her. Lynda had proven to him over and over again that she was no Justine Twyman. She wanted him, no strings attached. The more time he spent with her, the more he was convinced that she was different. She had put a major crack in his preconceived notion of a society lady. It had been close to twenty years that he'd carried that chip on his shoulder, but with Lynda, it all seemed silly, childish, a mistake of youth.

Tonight, after the fund-raiser, he planned to have a talk with her. The time had come to find out what she truly felt for him. The fund-raiser would be over. Tonight was either a beginning or an end. It was up to her.

As the chandelier lights flickered, indicating that the cocktail hour was over, Rico left to help Mrs. Ortiz round up the children for the trip home. Groups of people shuffled, drinks in hand, into the main ballroom. The room was jammed with tables, almost out into the hallway. Events, Inc. had outsold every other country club charity benefit this year with this fundraiser for Home Sweet Home.

Lynda was one of the last to leave, attempting, if not succeeding, to touch base with each and every guest personally. She made her way toward the dais by working the tables along the way. Glancing up at the raised table, she saw Rico climb the two steps and take a seat by Steve and Dee. He looked gorgeous in his black tuxedo—devilish, dangerous, devastatingly handsome—and her heart skipped a beat. She watched as he bantered back and forth with the Ballingers. He had to give a short speech tonight, yet he seemed relaxed. She, on the other hand, was as jumpy as a jackrabbit.

She'd persuaded Steve to give Rico the plaque and say a few words about the work of Home Sweet Home. Usually it was she who did the introduction for the guest of honor, but tonight, because of who he was, she'd relinquished the duty, knowing she would find it near impossible to praise him in public without choking up.

She found her seat next to the podium. Copies of the evening's program were stacked in front of her place setting, and she picked one up to leaf through it, checking to see that additional pledge cards were inserted.

The inside cover of the program had a long-shot photo of Home Sweet Home at the top, with a small insert picture of Rico and his staff. He had insisted that all the people who worked with him be included in the tribute, and she had agreed wholeheartedly.

After rearranging the programs, she picked up the donor pledge book and flipped through the various gold, silver and white embossed pages that displayed the good wishes and tributes to Home Sweet Home. It was during her second run through the pledge book that she felt a hand on her shoulder. Tilting back, she stared directly into Rico's eyes.

"Calm down," he said softly as he leaned over her.

"I am calm. Don't I look calm?"

"No, you look like you're ready to jump out of your skin."

"Well, maybe I'm just a little bit on edge. Aren't you the least bit nervous about speaking tonight?"

"No. I just picture everyone sitting out there in their underwear. It's very equalizing."

She shook her head at him and grinned. "You are a very sick man."

He brought his mouth to her ear and whispered, "You didn't say that this afternoon...."

Her face flushed to a cherry red. "You are not helping matters. Go back to your seat and behave," she said in her best schoolmarm voice.

Rico grinned and stroked her cheek, then took a step back toward his seat. "Bet you're not nervous anymore."

That was true. She was no longer nervous; she was embarrassed. His comment set off a kaleidoscope of images of her erotic performance earlier today. Never in her life had she been so... well...*loose,* as her mother would have said if she could have known—which, thank God, she couldn't.

Mother might not have been the most affectionate, loving person in the world, but she did bring Lynda up to be a lady. There were many words she might use to describe her behavior this afternoon, but *ladylike* was definitely not one of them.

An irrepressible, sly grin spread over her face, and her body shivered with the memory of it all. Yes, she was embarrassed, but also very pleased with herself. She had heard once, a long time ago, that there were no frigid women, only inept men. Recalling her sex life with her former husband, she was, without a doubt, living, breathing, unequivocal testimony to the truth of that wise adage.

Steve tapped Lynda's arm and broke into her reverie. They were ready to begin. Lynda took the podium and adjusted the microphone. She introduced herself and her organization and did a brief lead-in on the value of the fund-raiser before turning it over to Steve.

She sat as Steve took over, explaining the work of the shelter and its importance in the community. He ad-libbed wonderfully about his relationship with Rico, which set the tone with just the right touch of levity over and above the important issue of the homeless. Without too much fanfare, he introduced Rico to the crowd and presented him with a plaque of recognition for his work.

Lynda watched Rico's face as he accepted the award and shook hands with Steve. She could tell he was slightly amused by all this fuss, but a good enough sport to play along. He thanked Steve for a wonderful introduction and proceeded to give his speech about Home Sweet Home, and his dream to build a center for the homeless.

Lynda turned to observe the room. She'd heard the speech; they'd rehearsed it several times during the past few days. Her main interest was to see the crowd's reaction to his rather radical idea. Most faces were intent, some even nodded when he brought up a salient point or two, others fidgeted with their silverware or water glasses, anxious for the speeches to end and the party to resume.

It was a typical benefit crowd, she mused. You win some, you lose some. She was just about to return her attention to the podium when her peripheral vision caught sight of her ex-husband, Phillip, at a rear table to the far left. She felt an initial jolt of surprise, as if her memory of him had conjured him up. He had never attended any event she had sponsored in the past. Although she had made it a point to send invitations to his law firm, one of his partners always showed up in his place, which had suited her just fine.

It made her wonder why he was here tonight of all nights. It was hard to tell if his wife was with him, but then, it really didn't matter. She was gratified at the degree of indifference she felt about him or anything connected to him. Once, not so long ago, she thought, that would not have been the case. She would have been sitting here anxious and worried about her reaction to meeting him face-to-face. It was funny how one's perspective on life changed when one was in love. . . .

And she was in love. Absolutely. Irrevocably. Wholeheartedly. In love.

She looked up at Rico just as he was winding up his talk. His gaze met hers, and he smiled.

". . . And last but not least," he said to the crowd, "I would like to thank Ms. Lynda St. Clair. Not only for her hard work, but for her inspiration as well. There is a trite phrase, which is much overused, but tonight it applies too well to let that stop me . . ."

Rico held out his hand. Lynda took it and rose to stand next to him at the podium.

"Lynda, none of this would have been possible without you." He brushed his lips against hers. *"Muchas gracias, querida."*

A roar of applause arose from the crowd, initiated, no doubt by Dee, Steve and the rest of her unofficial committee who were so supportive. She knew she should be mortified by Rico's public display of affection—or more precisely, stamp of *ownership*—but she wasn't, not at all.

She turned and smiled at the crowd, advising them that the speeches were concluded for the evening. Another round of applause greeted that announcement, and everyone returned to their seats.

Lynda was glowing. Her face reflected her inner happiness much like a crystal ball. Though she had duties to perform as the evening wore on, she found that she couldn't keep her eyes off Rico for any significant length of time. She had a sneaking suspicion he felt the same way because whenever she sought him out, she found him looking at her.

At one point in time, he had whispered in her ear that he wanted to talk to her later. She'd agreed. They had things to settle. Her stomach rolled over at the thought of telling him about the donation, but she squelched the feeling. He would understand.

He would.

After dinner was served and the band began to play in earnest, she noticed Rico dancing with Jocelyn. As she turned to find Dee, she bumped head-on into Phillip.

"Whoa!" he said, and grabbed hold of her arm. "What's the hurry? Don't you have a hello for your ex?"

"Hello, Phillip. How are you?" she said with very little enthusiasm.

"Very well, thank you. Lovely affair. I hear great things about you, Lynda. Why don't you stop by our table. My wife is here. I'd like for you to meet her."

How annoying he is, she thought, but kept it to herself. "I hear she's pregnant, Phillip. Congratulations."

He graced her with a wide, pleased grin. It struck Lynda that he didn't even have the decency to feel embarrassed. Was he always such a pompous jerk?

"Yes, yes. One of the joys of marriage. Speaking of which...what about you? Getting married again?"

"No, why would you ask?" She looked over his shoulder in search of anyone to save her from further conversation with him.

"Oh, just wondering. You seem quite friendly with the guest of honor. I was just thinking that your taste in men seems to have...changed quite a bit."

She stared at the neat part in his blond hair, and wondered how in the world she'd ever thought herself in love with this bland man. One thing was certain, she'd be damned if she were going to discuss Rico with Phillip, not even for one minute.

"Oh, really, Phillip? What a coincidence. I was just thinking how very much it's *improved*." She disentangled her arm from his grasp. "You will excuse me, won't you? So nice to see you."

With a fake, but charming smile frozen on her face, Lynda pushed past him and weaved in between the dancers as she made her way toward Rico.

Rico had his hands full as well. Jocelyn was hanging all over him, using every beat of the music to insinuate her body against his. He had less than no interest in the woman. His attention was across the room on Lynda and the man she was talking to. He made no secret of his curiosity as he twisted and turned Jocelyn to gain a better view of the couple.

"Who is Lynda talking to?" he asked Jocelyn.

"Where? Oh, that's Phillip. Her ex."

A sharp, unexpected stab of jealousy shot through him. Rico watched as Lynda tossed off the man's grasp. She looked annoyed, defiant...bored. A wave of satisfaction quickly soothed the green-eyed dragon, and he smiled, sure of himself...and of her. His gaze followed her as she moved through the crowd in his direction.

The music slowed toward the end of the number, and Jocelyn wrapped both arms around Rico's neck. Absentmindedly he pulled her hands away.

"Why do I get the feeling I'm wasting my time?" Jocelyn asked out loud, not really expecting an answer. She seemed to be talking more to herself than to Rico, who was still too wrapped up with watching Lynda's every move to pay any attention to her.

Couples applauded the band as the song ended, and began to disperse just as Lynda arrived at Rico's side.

"Hi," she said, a bright, sincere smile of pleasure replacing the forced one.

"Hi, yourself," he said, grinning from ear to ear.

The music started again, and Lynda automatically slipped into his waiting arms.

"Don't mind me," Jocelyn said with a not-entirely-annoyed look on her face. She stood on the dance floor near them with her hands on her hips, then shrugged good-naturedly as she turned her back to them. "Oh, well," she said with an exaggerated sigh. "I know a lost cause when I see one."

Lynda thought she heard Jocelyn say something, but she wasn't sure. It couldn't be as important as the message she was receiving from Rico's heavy-lidded gaze. The dinner was drawing to a close, and the night loomed in front of them, thick with promise. She stood on her tiptoes and brushed her mouth against his, unmindful of the watchful eyes around them.

With each passing minute, the tension of the evening dissipated by degrees. Lynda felt her body loosen as his fingers kneaded the tight muscles between her shoulder blades and under the hair behind her neck.

She couldn't take her eyes off of his. His gaze roamed her face, as if he were looking, searching for something hidden beneath the surface.

"When can we get out of here?" he asked.

"Soon."

"How soon?"

"Right after the raffle," she said.

"When's that?"

"In about fifteen minutes. Can you wait that long?"

He turned her around to the beat of the music and discreetly pushed his hips into hers.

"Does that answer your question?"

"Oh, dear. Yes, I guess it does."

"Do it now," he said.

"Do what now?"

"The raffle."

"Okay. Right after this song."

They finished the dance in silence, bodies flush up against each other, yearning to be free of the restriction of clothing, of lights, of noise, of people.

Lynda led Rico toward the band's microphone, and announced the calling of the raffle prize winner. With much fanfare, the large silver punch bowl with all the tickets was brought up to them. Rico reached inside and pulled out a name, which Lynda read.

The winner was Megan Palmer.

The audience broke out in hysterical laughter at the coincidence. Meg's husband owned the car dealership that had donated the car. With a hand over her face to hide her embarrassment, Meg ambled up to the microphone to accept the prize.

"This is unbelievable!" she said. "All I can say is that I'm flabbergasted to be the winner." She ac-

cepted the keys from Lynda's outstretched hand, as
everyone applauded her.

As the band began playing the last song of the evening, Lynda excused herself to deal with the country
club management. After Lynda was gone, Megan
pulled Rico over to the side.

"I'll tell you what I'll do," she said to him in a low
voice. "I'm going to *re*donate the car. We'll wait a
while and have another raffle in the fall. How's that?"

"That's a very generous offer, Mrs. Palmer, but you
don't have to do that," Rico said. "You've done
enough for Home Sweet Home already."

"Oh, posh. I've done nothing!"

"You call your donation nothing?" Rico asked,
unable to hold back his sincere thanks any longer. "I
know you wanted it to be anonymous, but you must
know that without your help, we would not have been
able to get the plumbing fixed. We could have lost our
license. It was very generous indeed."

"Yes, it was. But I can't take the credit for it," Megan said.

"If you didn't make the donation, then who did?"

"Well, I really don't think it's my business to say,"
she hedged.

Rico felt a finger of cold dread trail up his spine.
"Say it anyway," he asked with little of the former
politeness in his voice.

"Mr. Alvarez, it's not up to me—"

"It's Lynda, isn't it?" he asked.

"I don't—"

"Yes or no."

Megan sighed, and bit her lip. "Yes. It was Lynda,
but you must understand—"

"Oh, I understand, Mrs. Palmer. Believe me, I understand everything very, very clearly. Thank you so much for your help." Rico smiled and led her away from the bandstand.

Lynda returned from signing the bills for the benefit. She offered her thanks to people as they were leaving, all the time searching over their heads for Rico. She found him, alone, leaning against the table in the corner of the room. He was preoccupied with yanking matches out of a matchbook with surgical precision and flipping them onto the tabletop.

He looked up as she approached. His eyes were intent, his face a mask of stone.

Uh-oh. Something was wrong. She recognized trouble when it looked her in the face, and trouble was staring at her right now. Her heart began to pound. There was only one thing between them that could cause such a look.

Her step faltered, and she swallowed hard. Rico pushed himself off the edge of the table and walked toward her.

"Are you ready?" he asked.

For what? she wondered. "Yes," she said.

He took hold of her arm, and she felt the tension in his fingers.

"Let's go," he said.

As she walked in front of him toward the door, she hardly acknowledged the compliments and congratulations of the few remaining stragglers who milled about on their way out. Her mind was blank, her plans for the rest of the night in disarray, and the only words that came to mind repeated themselves over and over again in a litany of dread.

He knows... He knows...

Ten

It was the longest twenty-minute ride of her life. Rico was quiet, calm, reserved...disturbingly so. She wished he'd do something—accuse her, scream at her—anything, instead of just complacently driving in silence, as if he were alone in the car, as if he were totally unbothered by what he'd heard, as if it didn't matter at all.

When they arrived at her house, she led the way inside, holding the door for him. Rico followed. Lynda flipped on the light switch and a soft yellow glow filled the room. The air was a bit stuffy, so she walked toward the patio doors and opened them. A cool ocean breeze drifted in, ruffling the voile curtains.

Behind her, Rico paced back and forth for a moment as if he were trying to decide what course of action to take. Lynda turned to him. Their eyes met, and he stopped pacing. Standing stock-still in the middle of the room, he placed his hands on his hips and studied her with intense concentration. He looked away and took off his tuxedo jacket. With meticulous care, he folded and placed it over the back of the sofa. He sat and shifted his body sideways in her direction.

Uncomfortable with the heavy silence, Lynda ambled across the room and sat on the chair across from him. Her throat was dry; she swallowed hard.

"I think the dinner went very well, don't you?" she asked.

"Very well," he said.

"It was a real surprise about Megan winning the car, wasn't it?"

"Quite. The night was full of surprises."

Lynda bit her lip. This was silly, ridiculous. They had to have it out, and it was obvious that she had to be the one to start it. *Go ahead, Lynda, don't be such a coward.*

"Is something bothering you?" she asked, unable to keep her mouth shut a minute longer.

"I don't know. Should something be bothering me?"

He wasn't a game player, yet here he was playing games with her. She couldn't handle this, not from him.

"You know, don't you." It wasn't a question.

"I know."

"Who told you?"

"Megan."

Lynda sighed. "Dee must have told her."

"Who else—besides me, that is—was in on this?" he asked.

"You make it sound like some sort of a conspiracy. It wasn't like that. It was a mistake."

"I'll say."

Lynda squeezed her eyes shut. "Don't..." she pleaded. "Don't act like this. Let me tell you what happened. Let me explain."

"What's to explain? That you went behind my back, explicitly against my wishes as if they didn't matter, and then told all your friends about it? Is that what you wish to explain to me?"

"Listen to me—"

He stood and paced in front of the sofa. "No. You listen to me. Listen to a little story I have to tell."

"I don't want to hear a story. I want to talk about this," she said.

"Oh, but you'll like this story. It's all about *this*. It's the story of a young man—a boy, really—who tried to take that great big step over the line."

"I don't know what you're talking about."

"He was nineteen, almost twenty, and he was so full of himself, it was inevitable that someone should knock him down a peg or two. Someone did. A woman. You know the type. A slick society blonde with a red Cadillac and a body that wouldn't quit." Rico laughed and ran his fingers through his hair. "Stupid kid, really. He fell in love. Hopelessly, starry-eyed in love. Bragged about her to his friends, his family, anyone who'd listen. Drove her in the Cadillac all around the neighborhood showing off how he'd come up in the world. You know, the kinds of things that appeal to guys that age. Macho things."

Rico walked over to her and leaned down, trapping her in the chair with an arm on each side. His black eyes were bright, sparkling with intensity. "You know what happened next?" he asked.

Lynda shook her head.

"No guess?"

"No."

"He asked her to marry him." He paused for a breath of a moment for her reaction. "It's okay, you can laugh if you want to. Go ahead."

"I don't want to laugh," she said softly.

"You don't? Well, *she* did. She laughed and laughed, so loud you could hear her in the next county. How droll, she said. You see, she was already engaged. To a *medical student*. Did he really think she would ever actually consider marrying *him?*"

Rico abruptly moved away from her. He walked over to the patio doors and leaned against them. For a long moment, he just stood there, staring out into the darkness. The wind picked up, and the back of his shirt caught it and billowed like a sail.

"He was good enough to go to bed with. Good enough to please her with his young, hot, Hispanic body, but not good enough to marry. No way, José. She was blueblood, Palm Beach, debutante. And he?" Rico shook his head and lowered his voice. "He was a fool."

Lynda stood and walked up behind him. "What happened to the boy?" She had to hear the end, let him finish, get it all out, once and for all.

"He quit school. Joined the Marines. Went to 'Nam. The usual for someone in those days with a messed-up head."

She was consumed with compassion for the heart-broken boy he once was. Knowing him as she did, she knew how it must have been for him then—the deep, irrevocable hurt, the blow to his Latin pride, the embarrassment in front of his family and friends. He would have had to get away from it all, to run, to hide, to lick his wounds.

Lynda touched his arm. He turned and looked at her over his shoulder.

"Just so that you don't think it was a total loss, she did give him the car. That shiny, red Cadillac." His mouth curved with a derisive grin. "Payment. For services rendered."

Her hand slipped from his arm as Rico moved away without touching her. Silently she watched as he picked up his jacket and put it on.

"Where are you going?" she asked.

"Home."

"No," she said. "Not yet."

He looked up at her expectantly.

"You've told your story, now it's my turn to tell mine."

"I don't want to hear about how you did this for my own good, Lynda. I can't live with your money buying things for me, *buying me*. And you've proved you don't respect my feelings on that issue. What's left to say?"

"Sit down."

He stared at her, annoyed with her damned, cool, autocratic attitude.

"It's my turn, Rico. Let me have my say. Then, if you still want to leave, I won't stop you."

He blew out a breath he didn't realize he was holding and lifted his shoulders in a studied shrug of forced resignation. He sat on the edge of the sofa, draping his jacket across his knees, an indication that he didn't intend to stay very long.

"Talk."

"I have a story, too," she said. "It's about a girl, you might call her a typical poor little rich girl. It's sad, but true, you know." She took a deep cleansing breath and lifted her chin. "There really are people like that. People who have children, then leave them alone to be raised by strangers in a variety of houses throughout the world. People who should never have children at all, who are totally selfish and into themselves." She shrugged. "But they do. For whatever reasons, they have these babies, and they do leave them all alone to grow up following whatever blueprint they've left with the nannies, tutors, servants and boarding school teachers they've hired."

Lynda sighed and shut her eyes. "How can I make you understand? You, who have this loving family, this community of friends? You couldn't possibly know what it's like to live with people who are *paid* to be kind to you, to nurse you when you're sick, to praise you when you've done something wonderful." She put her head down and studied her hands. "To say they love you, all for the right price."

She walked over and sat next to him on the sofa. Rico's face was somber, and his jaw set in anger. But he wasn't angry with her anymore. He was angry with her parents who had hurt her so by their indifference. She'd told him when they'd first met that neglect had many faces. He'd questioned her ability to know about such things. He understood now, and his heart was splitting in two, for God help him, no matter what she did to him or how she lied to him, he couldn't deny the fact that he loved her. A knot had formed in his stomach, growing larger and tighter with each word she'd uttered. He reached out and took hold of her hand.

Lynda looked down at her hand in his. She slowly drew circles around each of his knuckles with her index finger. Without looking up at him, she continued, "I learned very early in life that money was a tool to be used to get what you wanted. I never thought of the donation as 'buying you.' It never entered my mind. I wanted to help you." She looked up at him, and he saw the tears pooled in her eyes. "I wanted to show you how much I loved you in the only way I knew how."

Rico cradled her face in the palms of his hands. He reached out with his thumbs to wipe the tears from the corners of her eyes. His face was contorted with myriad emotions—the pain he felt for both their young hurts combined with the love he felt now for this woman who was his in every way he could imagine.

"Don't . . ." he whispered. "Don't cry. Not for me. Not for that little girl long ago. She's gone. She's a beautiful, caring woman now . . . a woman like no other . . . a woman I love with all my heart."

He bent his head and kissed her. She parted her tremulous lips and accepted the thrust of his tongue into the deep recesses of her mouth. Their breaths mingled, warming them, melting the icy chill that had clutched at their hearts just minutes ago.

Lynda clung to his forearms, digging her nails into the material of his shirt, bunching the starched cotton in her hands. She kissed him back with all the love she had buried for so long.

Their lips parted, but they remained in each other's embrace. Rico stared at her tear-stained face. Gently he kissed one cheek, then the other.

"I want to touch you, make love with you right now," he whispered, "More than I've ever wanted anything ever before."

They walked arm in arm into the master bedroom. The satin comforter on the bed was bathed with a pale moonglow from the skylight overhead. Rico unzipped her dress and let it fall to her feet. She was braless, and her breasts gleamed in the moonlight. Rico ran the back of his hand across the tips and watched as they instantly puckered at his touch.

Cupping one in each hand, he bent his head to take the pouting orbs into his mouth, but Lynda intercepted him. She entwined her fingers in his hair and brought his lips to hers. She kissed him with her mouth open wide under his, boldly thrusting her tongue inside, holding him still with the power of her kiss.

Lynda drew away, her mouth wet and swollen from the assault. She unhooked each stud from each buttonhole of his dress shirt with unerring precision. She pushed the shirt open and splayed her palms against the hard muscles of his chest. Leaning into him, she kissed his warm skin, rubbing her cheek against him, lingering at the spot over his heart. She smiled into his flesh, rejoicing at the thought that every beat of his heart was for her.

Rico reached down and unsnapped her garter belt. He insinuated his hands into the elastic band of her bikini panties and captured her bottom with both hands. He lifted her slightly off the ground, massaging the rounded flesh as he brought her body up against his. One hand dipped between her legs, and he touched her intimately from behind, reveling in the wet heat his fingers encountered.

Lynda arched her back as his fingers worked their magic, unable and unwilling to move lest he stop this divine torment. When she could stand no more, she backed away, and led him to the bed. Her body was on fire with the heat of passion and the depth of her love for him. She was impatient to feel him on her, in her, wrapped around her.

She stepped out of her panties and lay down on the comforter, clad only in her white stockings and un-clipped garter belt. With one knee raised, and the other leg dangling off the bed, Lynda opened her body to his view. The glow from the moon filtered through the skylight. The blond curls between her legs glis-tened with a silvery aura—inviting, beckoning, taunt-ing him to come closer, touch, taste, feel all she had to offer.

Rico quickly shed the rest of his clothing and knelt between her legs. His blood was pulsing through his veins at an alarming speed, and he leaned above her, muscles tight and arms strained on either side. The tip of his arousal skimmed the skin of her belly. Lynda reached down to touch him with featherlike caresses. With a boldness borne of love, she wrapped her fin-gers around his thickness and stroked him until he shouted her name with a plea and a warning.

Rico shut his eyes and rested his weight on her for a long moment. She welcomed the feel of him flush against her. He was so hot, so hard, she couldn't stop touching him—his hair, his neck, the taut muscles of his back. They were so close, she couldn't tell where his body ended and hers began.

He shimmied to nestle himself within the cradle of her hips. With slow, sure strokes, he rubbed himself against her. Lynda whimpered. She was melting down into a puddle of want, with no will of her own, only instinct guiding her now, searching for the ultimate fulfillment she craved more than anything.

She fidgeted under him, until he could take no more. He drove into her with one soul-shattering thrust, and brought them home.

Her body stretched to accommodate him as naturally as if they were two parts of a puzzle. He moved within her, slowly at first, but then passion overcame reason, and they were lost in a world of their own making. With each stroke of his body, he told her he loved her. With each movement of her hips she said the same.

Rico kissed her so deeply, she thought he might devour her whole. They linked hands, fingers entwined, mouths fused together as their bodies caught an almost frantic rhythm. Lynda wrapped her legs around his, digging her heels into him as an explosive climax gripped her and spun her to dizzying heights. Rico absorbed the shock and climbed a mountain of his own, until he, too, found his release. His heart pounded in his chest, his breath caught in his throat, and his body gave up the battle to the pleasure of love.

They didn't speak for a long time. There was very little left to say that their bodies hadn't already communicated to each other with an eloquence beyond words.

Lynda felt as if a weight had been lifted from her shoulders. She felt light, unencumbered, as free as a caged tiger just returned to the wild. Her mind was full of energy, but her body was spent. The tensions of the evening had taken their toll, and she felt herself drifting off.

Rico pulled the comforter over them, and turned her body spoon-style into his. His arm supported her head and his hand cupped her breast.

"I love you," she whispered into the dark silence.

He kissed her hair and his arm tightened around her. "I love you, too, *querida*. So much. So very much."

"Rico—"

"Shh . . . Go to sleep. Tomorrow. We'll talk tomorrow."

He pushed a leg between hers, and she nestled her bottom against him. He knew the moment she fell asleep. Her hand slipped off his and her body slumped against him. He tightened his hold on her and breathed in her special scent, closing his eyes with the feelings it evoked.

Thoughts swirled through his head. He should be tired, but he was not. He had never been more wide-awake in his life. His body was taut, not only with the wonder of their love, but with the uncertainty as to what it all meant. He couldn't stop asking himself "What now?"

He forcibly shut his eyes and tried to sleep. At some time during the night, he must have dozed because when he opened his eyes again, Lynda was facing him, her head on his chest, her body sprawled across his. He rubbed the stubble on his chin with the palm of his hand and yawned. The sky above was lightening; it was just before dawn.

Rico shifted, and Lynda murmured in her sleep. He pulled himself out from beneath her ever so gently so as not to wake her. He stood in the cool morning air and covered her with the comforter. She instinctively snuggled down into its warmth. With a guarded touch, he brushed the hair back from her face, and tenderly kissed her brow as he might do for one of the children at the shelter. For that was the way he thought of her now: as belonging to him, cherished, loved and protected by him and all he deemed holy.

He walked to the closet and pulled out a pair of his jeans that he had left earlier. He slipped them on without snapping or zipping them. Barefoot, he walked back into the living room and turned off the lamp. The patio doors were still open, but the wind had died down during the night with only a light breeze heralding the new dawn.

Stepping out onto the deck, he felt the cool wood beneath his feet. He walked toward the railing and leaned his elbows down on it. A yellow-orange halo skimmed the horizon to the east, casting a fire's glow on the water. It was morning cool, and he was shirtless. Goose pimples broke out on his skin, but he didn't go back inside. The air felt good, made him feel alive, made him feel that anything was possible.

Was it? Was anything possible if you wanted it enough? Lynda loved him; he didn't doubt that for one minute. But there was still who she was and what she was to be dealt with. His lot in life was chosen. It might seem selfish, but it was she who had all the decisions to make. It was she who had to give things up, and so, ultimately, where they went from here was entirely up to her.

He wanted to ask her to marry him. His dream was to have her at his side, doing what she did so well: fund-raising. Once he got the center off the ground, that would be a full-time job unto itself, one that she'd more than proven she was a thousand times more qualified to handle than he. But would it be enough for her? He shook his head. He didn't know. He didn't know how deep her love was, and part of him was afraid to test it, especially now, when it was all so new and so fragile.

The sun rose by degrees, at first only a crescent of light, then a half, until slowly the entire orange ball filled the sky with the bright beginning of a new day.

Rico shifted his weight from one foot to the other and surveyed his surroundings. How would she feel about giving all this up? The commitment he was asking her to make was a total and complete turn-around from everything she'd ever known. She loved him, but how much? That much?

His problem was, he just didn't know.

Lynda swung her arm out as she turned in the bed. In her sleepy state, she felt around with her hand and encountered empty space. Her eyes slowly opened, and she blinked at the brightness of the light filtering in from the skylight overhead.

Lifting her head, she looked around. Where had Rico gone? An instant of panic washed over her, and she sat up. The comforter fell to her waist. She rubbed her hands over her arms to ward off the chill of the morning air. Leaving the bed, she pulled her long terry robe off the hook behind the bathroom door and wrapped herself inside it, tying the belt tightly around her waist.

She walked into the living room and looked around. Thinking he might be in the kitchen, she made her way toward that room when her peripheral vision caught him out on the deck. He was standing quietly staring into the sunrise. A swell of emotion closed her throat at the sight of his perfect profile. She loved him so much, it hurt.

Running her fingers through her hair to try to smooth out the tangles, she padded barefoot outside. Coming up behind him, she wrapped her arms around him and laid her head on his back.

"Good morning," she said, and kissed him between the shoulder blades.

Without turning to her, he answered, "Good morning, *querida*. Did you sleep well?"

"Mmm...very well." She scratched her fingernails into the curls in the center of his chest. "How about some breakfast?" she asked.

"Maybe later."

Lynda lifted her head and tilted it. She stared at his profile. His face looked tired, serious. She'd thought they'd worked out all their differences last night, but there was something else bothering him. She could almost feel it in his body.

"What is it? What's wrong?"

"Nothing's wrong," he said softly.

"Yes, there is. I can feel it in you."

Rico lowered his gaze and smiled. Her perceptions of him were too good, as if they were so in tune with each other that anything affecting him, no matter how small or insignificant, was magnified and reflected in her.

"I have something to ask you," he said softly. "But I don't want you to answer me now. I want you to think about it, really think it over carefully. Then, when you've taken the time, you can give me your answer."

"What do you want to ask me?" Lynda held her breath, hoping against hope it was the one question, the only question in the world she wanted to hear from him.

"I want to ask you to marry me."

Lynda tightened her hold on him for the tiniest of moments, then let go. She moved around and leaned her back against the deck railing to look him in the eye.

"Are you asking me?"

"Yes. I'm asking you. Will you marry me?"

"Yes."

Rico shook his head. "Not so fast. I told you I don't want an answer today. I want you to think about it."

"There's nothing to think about. Yes."

"Lynda, be reasonable. You know what I'm about to do. You know the commitment you'd be making. Your entire life-style is in jeopardy here. And there's no turning back. If you marry me, it's forever. I'll never let you go."

"I'll never want to go. Yes."

He took her shoulders in his hands and gave her a chiding shake. "Listen to me. You have a company to think about, your friends, the country club, this house for heaven's sake. You're just going to give it all up." He snapped his fingers in the air over her head. "Just like that?"

"Yes."

"You're crazy."

"Yes. Absolutely *loco*. About you."

Rico stared at her long and hard. He shook his head, and his mouth curved into a half smile. "I thought this was going to be so hard."

"Why would you think that? I love you. I love everything *about* you. I am *in* love with you. There isn't anything in the world that's more important to me than that.'' She cupped his face with her palm, and her eyes filled with tears of joy. ''Rico, I've had every possible thing in this world that money can buy. The only thing I've never had is the one thing that I've wanted most of all. To belong to someone. To be loved for me, myself, not because someone was paid to do it, but because they just did.''

She moved into him and brushed her lips against his.

''Do you love me?'' she asked.

''With all my heart.''

Lynda wrapped her arms around his neck. Rico enfolded her in his embrace. With the early-morning sun shining up above, she buried her face in his neck.

''Then that's all I'll need. Forever.''

* * * * *

Silhouette Desire

COMING NEXT MONTH

DOMINIC
Lass Small

Dominic Lorenzo saw Fiona Evans and wanted her. He even used his little boy to keep her near. But eventually Fiona realized that Dominic was keeping something from her. What could he have done that was so terrible?

MAN FROM COUGAR PASS
Barbara McCauley

Cassie Phillips came to Cougar Pass to find her wayward younger sister and to prevent her from making a horrible mistake. But, when Slade Mason said the only way she could get to Sarah was to hike through the forest with him, Cassie wondered who would save *her*?

KNIGHT AND DAY
Carole Buck

Donna Day worked at a home for abused children and she saw a look in comedian Marty Knights' eyes that reminded her of those children. But she had a secret past too, and she knew Marty hadn't dealt with his. Could he?

COMING NEXT MONTH

CAST ADRIFT
Donna Carlisle

Jess Seward and Kelsey Morgan were the original irresistible force and immovable object. Two weeks at sea while Kelsey completed her dolphin research were going to seem never ending, especially after that first night together!

PHILLY AND THE PLAYBOY
Linda Turner

Morgan Stewart had good looks, good genes and a sizeable bank account, so it was no wonder that some of his constituents thought that he was as much a playboy as a politician. Philadelphia O'Neil challenged him to spend time in a shelter for the homeless. How would he cope?

THE CASE OF THE MESMERIZING BOSS
Diana Palmer

The first book in Diana Palmer's exciting new series in Desire.

Dane Lassiter had his own firm of private detectives but when his secretary needed protection, no one else would do. . .